HEARTS COLLIDE IN BEDPA VALLEY
BOOK 1

DEVON COOK

Camouflage Hearts

Hearts Collide in Bedpa Valley Book One

Interior images by mgsdesiigns

Windbound Legacy

Of Wind and Shadows

Hearts Collide in Bedpa Valley

Camouflage Hearts

Contents

To those who've loved quietly from the sidelines, who waited, hoped, and stayed—even when it hurt.
This is for the hearts that never gave up.

Camouflage Hearts explores themes of military affiliation and the profound impact of death during deployment and PTSD that may follow.

If you or someone you know is struggling with PTSD, depression, or anxiety related to military service, resources like the **Veterans Crisis Line** (Dial 988, then press 1), **VA Mental Health Services,** or **Give An Hour** (giveanhour.org) offer confidential support and care.

Take care of yourselves and each other.

And then there was only you—
suddenly and unexpectedly,
but right on time.
- M. M. McNeely

Chapter One

Seven Years Ago - New Years Eve

"I'M NOT GOING," Willa groaned as she plopped down on her bed.

Her best friend of fifteen years, Sofia, stood in the bathroom applying *another* coat of mascara. She blinked a few times before leaning back to turn her attention on Willa, rolling her bright blue eyes in the process. "You need to get out and have some fun."

Willa chewed on her lip as she watched Sofia put her mascara down on the counter before she turned to sit down on the bed, her dyed black hair curled and swishing around her shoulders with every step she took. As she sat down, Sofia cupped Willa's cheeks, her eyes blazing with determination and just under-the-surface worry. "I love you, girl. But you *need* to get out and be twenty-two for a chance."

Yeah, I know. "I haven't been in the mood to go out. Not everyone wants to go out, Sof. It's completely normal."

"No, it's not. Not for *why* you're doing it." Willa opened her mouth to argue, but was cut off. "Cooper left you almost a year ago. You grieved, then sulked. Now you're just downright avoiding moving on." Sofia's eyes bore into Willa.

Feeling defensive, Willa pulled her head back out of Sofia's grip. "That's not true."

"Please." She crossed her arms. "Then tell me why you don't want to go tonight."

Why *did* she not want to go? She really had no reason; she *should* get out and do things people her age did, but she wasn't about to tell Sofia that the breakup with Cooper really fucked her up. Or tell her the fact that she's cried herself to sleep more than she cared to admit, and it was *just* now starting to not feel as painful. She finally felt like she could do what she needed to do—focus on her life and her military career.

After her breakup with Cooper blindsided her, she decided she needed to focus on anything other than men. If she didn't focus on men, then she wouldn't have to worry about the numbness again.

When she didn't answer, Sofia sighed. "Please. Come with us tonight. We'll make Cruz be the third wheel."

Willa smiled at the comment, knowing that was *exactly* what Sofia's fiancée would do. Cruz was a complete godsend freshman year of college after the shit Sofia's ex put her through in high school. He treated her like the Queen she was and healed the jagged pieces of her heart. It was one of the things Willa loved most about him.

"It's New Year's Eve, Sof. I don't want to go and make him play third wheel. It's a fresh start—"

Sofia cut her off, "*Exactly*. It's a fresh start. Wash away the old, welcome in the new, or whatever our parents say. Come on. Let's go out and have some fun. You never know, maybe you'll meet someone."

Willa scoffed. "I am *not* hooking up with someone tonight. That is such a cliché."

Sofia laughed. "I didn't say hook up. Knowing you, you'd end up pregnant." Willa let out a laugh because she knew she was right. That would be her luck.

"Fine." She said after a moment. She did need to get out of the apartment. "I'll go."

"Thank *fuck*." She stood abruptly, walking to the closet to grab the short, velvet maroon dress she brought with her. "Put this on. We need to get going. The party starts at eleven." She dropped the dress on the bed before leaving the room.

Willa glanced at the clock, seeing it was only ten-thirty. The party was only a few blocks away, so they could easily walk and be there on time. When Sofia shut the door behind her, Willa stood, stripping out of her fleece pajamas, tossing them on the bed next to the dress, before she grabbed a strapless black bra and matching thong from the dresser. She walked to the bathroom to check the damage to her appearance.

"I'm a fucking mess." She muttered to herself.

Willa's chestnut brown hair was pulled up in a messy bun, and the day-old mascara that she failed to clean off after work was smudged, but easily fixable. She let out a sigh as she pulled the hair tie out, running her fingers through her hair as it fell around her shoulders. Her hair wasn't that bad, but there was a clear indentation from where the hair tie sat.

Shit. She didn't have time to hop in the shower to wash her hair, not with Sofia stressing over the time. She grabbed the discarded hair tie, throwing her hair back up in a loose bun, before using pins to clean it up some, giving the illusion she spent hours on it, instead of mere seconds. She grabbed some tendrils of wavy hair, letting them cascade around her face.

Satisfied with that, she grabbed a cotton round and her makeup remover to clean up the smudged mascara. When she was happy with the results, Willa picked up the closest eyeshadow palette—one that held six shades of matte and shimmery taupe—before selecting the softest option that would look nice, but also make her dark green eyes pop. She wanted to keep it simple, so she could come home and, *hopefully,* remove the makeup with ease so she could drop into bed.

Stepping back, she turned left to right, checking angles to make sure she was satisfied with her hair and makeup.

Willa walked back into the bedroom, grabbed the soft velvet dress, stepped into it, reveling in the way the fabric felt against her skin. *Thank God I shaved today*.

She pulled the zipper up as she stepped into the living room, where she found her best friend sitting on the blue couch, staring at two pairs of heels.

"What are you doing?" She asked while she placed a simple pair of opal drop earrings for a hint of glamor.

"I'm trying to decide which shoes to wear." She ran her hands over her dark green dress; her engagement ring sparkled in the light.

Willa sat down next to her friend, studying the two sets of glorious heels. The black ones on the left were peep-toe booties with a cutaway heel. The cream heels were a classic sole silhouette with a slender toe band

and adjustable ankle straps. "The black ones would go better with your dress, I think."

Sofia nodded in agreement. "That's what I was thinking too," she reached for the booties. "The cream color with that dress is going to be *killer*. Maybe you'll get a midnight kiss because of them." Willa rolled her eyes as she slipped the shoes on.

As she secured the second heel, Cruz walked in. The man looked like he walked straight out of a nineties movie; his black hair hung in his face, like Leonardo DiCaprio's did in *Titanic*. For some men, it would make them look arrogant, but for Cruz, it just added to his essence. Sofia jumped up, running straight into his arms and planting a kiss on his lips.

Willa sat back, letting out a sigh, wishing she had someone to be excited about again. Cooper had gotten along with Sofia and Cruz, had blended with them seamlessly, as if he had always been a part of their group, not that he stuck around. When the breakup happened, she thought her friendships were over, Cooper stealing them from her.

Not in the mindset to watch them act like they didn't live together, Willa turned her attention toward the sliding door, where the lights of Hetbay glowed in the night sky. She loved them both and loved that they finally found happiness together, but it was like a knife in her chest every time they were together and glowing with happiness.

"Come on, Willa," Sofia said, oblivious to her friend's inner turmoil. She stood and followed them to the door, locking up as she stepped outside.

THEY WALKED THE three blocks to Club Thirst, Sofia doing her best to keep Willa from trailing behind. "We should've driven," she whined.

Cruz laughed as he threw his arms around his fiancée's shoulders once they entered the elevator, just inside the doors of the club. "Sof, I parked the car here earlier, so we didn't have to walk back. I have work tomorrow, so I'm not planning on drinking, and we can go home."

Sofia pouted but sent a smile to Willa. "Do you have work tomorrow? I forgot to ask." The hum of the elevator moving filled the space for a moment.

Willa shook her head. "No. The squadron was given tomorrow off because of the holiday. I have to go back on the second, though." She grumbled, not looking forward to it. She was supposed to spend the week shadowing the fire department, around people she was not very fond of. All she wanted to do was sit at her desk.

"Ahh, good! Then we'll spend the day together!" Sofia bounced in her heels. Willa cringed, hoping her friend wasn't going to topple over.

"As long as you don't wake me up at five to go running, I'm fine with that." She didn't mind running but wasn't about to go out of her way to run on a holiday off.

They stepped off the elevator to the rooftop restaurant and bar as Willa decided she would only have two drinks and try to enjoy herself. She knew she needed to, needed to move past this depression cloud that seemed to hang over her every day. Limiting the drinks would also prevent her from having a hangover from hell, on top of the inevitability of being socially drained.

Cruz led them to a reserved table, one he must've snagged when he dropped his car off. *Thank God.* She didn't want to have to alternate who could leave the table and who had to babysit.

"Do you mind holding my keys?" She asked him. "I forgot to grab a bag, and I don't want to risk losing them."

"Not at all," he took the keys when she held them out and stuck them in his belt loop for safekeeping.

"Thanks." She smiled at him before he grabbed Sofia's hand, pulling her to him. He kissed her temple before speaking. "I want to dance with you, Sweets."

Sofia looked at Willa. "Are you okay with that?"

She rolled her eyes and held up the reserved sign that read *Pendola, Cruz.* "I don't have to babysit the table, and I can try to mingle. I'll be fine." Willa shooed them away.

Before Sofia could say more, Cruz pulled his fiancée to the dance floor, spinning her as she squealed when her favorite song, "Everytime We Touch," started. She belted the lyrics out as she clung to Cruz.

She's such a dork, Willa thought as she made her way to the bar.

"Is this seat taken?" She asked a blonde woman to her left. She turned and smiled. "Nope. All yours."

"Thanks," Willa said as she slid onto the empty stool. The woman had already turned her attention to whoever she was in conversation with. Not minding the immediate brush-off, Willa placed her hands on the bar to adjust her balance.

She waited patiently for the bartender to make his way to her. She had decided her New Year's resolution would be to ease into a social life, even though she knew it wouldn't stick.

The blonde woman next to her slid off her stool and walked away. Willa released a breath of relief when she was hit with a mouthwatering scent of coastal citrus, sea mist, and clean wood. She closed her eyes, savoring the scent. It was the same one she begged Cooper to wear, but he decided to wear it only on special occasions.

She turned, half expecting—hoping—to see his brown eyes staring back at her, full of regret for tearing her heart into pieces.

The man who came with the smell was *definitely* not Cooper. His tall, muscular frame loomed over her, donned in all black; his neatly styled brown hair fell in a sleek quiff. Their gazes met, revealing his captivating cerulean eyes. Beneath a day's growth of stubble, his jawline was defined and robust. A straight, well-proportioned nose complemented his high cheekbones, crafting a distinctly handsome profile. He looked like a damn God.

Holy shit. She felt her knees tremble, enough to know that if she wasn't already sitting, she would've been instantly. This man was devastatingly handsome.

He smiled at her, making her heart flutter. *Oh my.* "Mind if I sit?" he asked, his voice huskier than she expected.

She shook her head, unsure if she was capable of talking at this point. *Get it together, Willa.*

He sat on the empty stool and extended a hand. "Declan Hawke."

"Willa Evans." She said, gripping his hand, soaking in his warmth and strength. Her heart pounded. *I really need a drink.*

She turned her attention back to the bar as the bartender stepped their way. *Thank you, God.*

"What can I get for you?" He asked as he stopped in front of her.

"Mmm, strawberry daiquiri, please." She answered. The bartender nodded once as his eyes slid to Declan's. She needed cold and sweet, anything to cool the heat coursing through her.

"Whiskey, thanks." When the bartender walked away, Willa studied him through the mirror placed behind the shelves of alcohol.

He was way too attractive for his own good, and hers. She shifted on her stool, heat starting to pool low in her belly. It's been almost a year since she felt this way last. Was one brief meeting *really* getting her blood pumping?

What is wrong with me? An attractive man sits next to me, and all of a sudden, I'm turned on.

She crossed her legs, hoping to ease *some* of the pressure that had built.

As if he sensed it, his blue eyes locked onto hers through the mirror. Her entire body went rigid. She wanted to turn to him, but couldn't bring herself to do it. Willa let out a shaky breath, and the fucker *smirked.*

Oh. This wasn't good. She needed to get out of there. She *needed* her legs to move.

A body walked in front of them, forcing their eye contact to be cut off. She blinked a few times, processing what was happening. The bartender had slid their drinks in front of them and was already walking away by the time Willa figured it out.

"Fuck. I didn't pay him." She muttered. Declan's body shook slightly from holding in a laugh. She looked at him. "What's so funny?"

"You were so caught up in the moment you hadn't realized I paid for our drinks." His eyes sparkled like the ocean at sunrise.

"Why would you pay for my drink?" she looked at the glass, then, bunched her eyebrows together. "I can take care of myself." Cooper had never once bought her a drink in all the time they had been together. It didn't make sense to her, so why would Declan?

When he said nothing, she looked at him again. He studied her, an eyebrow arched in question at her. "Have you never had a guy buy you a drink?"

"I—" she closed her mouth, looking up to the clear sky, willing away the tears that threatened to fall. *Shit, not now.*

"Oh God, Willa. I'm sorry. *Fuck.*" The last word was barely audible. He dragged his hands over his face. "I was just trying to do something nice for an attractive woman."

As his words hit her, she fully looked at him. "You find me attractive?" Surely he was joking. No one ever called her attractive. Even Cooper had rarely said the words or made me feel that way.

The realization of that hit her like a ton of bricks. Cooper hadn't told her he found her attractive for a solid year before they broke up, she was sure of it.

Declan's eyes met hers; they had darkened to a tempest. Why the hell was she questioning this?

Just shut up, Willa.

Chapter *Two*

"YOU'RE KIDDING, RIGHT?" Declan asked. The woman was absolutely insane for questioning this. He had come to this party because his coworker and best friend, Maddox, had convinced him. He didn't want to be out of the apartment, but he figured a New Year's Eve party was a good opportunity to mingle, God knows he needed it, especially since he was most likely being sent overseas again. When he caught Willa and her two friends walking into the club, he felt a shift, some sort of pull towards this dark-haired woman. He had clapped Maddox on the back—a silent thank you for making him come out.

Willa stared at him, bewilderment in her eyes, giving him the chance to get lost in them. How could she seriously think he wouldn't find her attractive?

He shifted in the stool, turning towards her, their knees brushing, as he took in her body, the soft curves he was dying to run his hands over. "I'm going to be completely honest with you." He paused, allowing the tension to build, reveling in the way she squirmed in her seat, the soft hitch in her breath. Sure, women fawned over him plenty, but he had never felt this pull towards any of them. Her big, green eyes pulled him in like a siren to a sailor, but her lips. *Fuck.*

Every fantasy he'd ever had was rolled into this one woman.

"I have never been more serious in my life."

She laughed, the sound overtaking his very soul. She brightened so much that he found himself craving to get her to laugh more, to smile. "I don't believe you."

He flashed her a wicked grin. "You don't believe that I'm being this serious, or that I find you attractive?"

She arched an eyebrow at him. "Both." Her eyes sparked with a challenge; one he was definitely on board with proving. He had never been challenged like this before, between the touch of her knee against his still, and that look. His blood simmered with need.

He looked around at the other patrons and noticed a few men constantly stealing glances her way, the look of want on their faces. "You are most definitely the most attractive woman in this place. As for my seriousness," he straightened his back and held out his hand to her again. "Let's start fresh. I'll give you a taste of what I'm really like."

She studied his hand before playing along, slipping her hand into his. He pulled her hand to his lips, pressing a kiss to her knuckles. He heard the small gasp that escaped from her pouty lips. He smirked as he looked at her. "I was feeling a little off today—but you've turned me on again."

She threw her head back and laughed. Declan smiled, still holding onto her hand, his thumb tracing small circles over her knuckles. She smelled like lavender and amber, and he wanted to lick her up and devour her.

Her green eyes found his again, the playfulness in them both with teasing and a deep want that—*fuck*. He wanted to get on his knees for her. "Please tell me that line has never worked for you."

Feigning hurt, he dropped her hand. "No, never. But it got a laugh out of you, so I feel like I've won."

When she took the opportunity to grab her drink, he did the same. His heart was pounding in his chest. She hadn't dismissed him yet, so something had to be working. He wondered if it could keep working, and he could find out if she tasted as sweet as her drink.

"Are you a murderer?" She asked as the whiskey slid down his throat. He coughed, caught off guard.

"What?" He set the glass down carefully.

"Are you a murderer? Or a psycho?" he looked at her and studied her face. She was dead serious.

"Uhm—no. No, I'm not either of those things." Maybe she was the crazy one.

She tapped a nail against her glass as if weighing her next words. "If we were in a relationship and I was kidnapped," *where the fuck was she going with this?* "Would you let me go, or would you hunt down my kidnappers and threaten their lives?"

"Why are you asking this?" He needed to know. This was not how he expected the conversation to go.

"Just answer the question. Humor me." The emerald depths of her eyes swam with something he couldn't quite place.

Fine, I'll play. "Serious relationship?"

She smiled at him. "Of course. Say on the verge of engagement."

Declan lifted an eyebrow at her at the sudden change of hypothetical. "Oh, well, in that situation, yes. I'd pull a *where's my wife* move. You'd be mine, and mine *only*." He growled out the last word, suddenly feeling like he wanted to protect this strange creature in front of him.

Willa shifted in her seat as her beautiful face flushed, and he watched her bite her plump lip. *Oh yeah, I definitely nailed that one.* She cleared her throat, causing him to mask his face to hide the smirk that threatened to show itself. "Okay. You pass. Come on." She grabbed her drink as she stood. Declan took in her long legs displayed deliciously just under the hem of the maroon dress, hugging those soft, ample curves.

He slid off the stool, grabbing his whiskey. He extended his elbow, through which she slid her hand effortlessly through the gap. She felt like she was made to be on his arm. He felt his heart start to race at the idea of her always being on his arm.

She guided him towards a reserved table, the name *Pendola, Cruz* written on a pristine white card. A small hint of jealousy coursed through his veins at the male name. He waited for her to sit before taking the seat beside her. His stomach bunched up with nerves, so he took another sip of whiskey to hopefully alleviate them. *Why am I getting so nervous sitting here with her?* He had been just fine at the bar; it was like here at this table, everything felt more concrete, fuller. He wouldn't lie and say that a large part of him was enjoying that feeling, even if the nerves threatened.

Willa shifted in her seat to face him as he set the glass down. Declan leaned forward and placed his hand along the back of her chair, his calloused thumb grazing her arm in the motion. She sucked in a breath at the contact as his own heart skipped a beat.

God, what is this woman doing to him? He never got jittery over women; usually, he was the one making the woman jittery. He watched her; everything about her was different than what he had expected, and he craved more.

She opened her mouth to say something, but closed it again. "What is it?" He didn't care what happened after tonight; whether they never spoke again or this whatever it was became something, but he wanted her to know she could trust him. *No,* that wasn't true. He couldn't end the night without her knowing she had his trust. It was just who he was.

"I just wanted to say," she paused, chewed on her lip. What he would fucking give to stop her from doing that, to run his thumb across her lip. "I had a very serious relationship, and earlier this year, it ended. I was blindsided, and I—I haven't gotten over it. Not really." She turned her head, no doubt to see where her friends were. As if she were worried, they would suddenly appear and hear her.

"Friends don't know this?" he asked.

Her green eyes locked onto his, swimming with emotions that added to the knots in his stomach. "No, they don't." She took a drink and swallowed it before setting the glass down. "How'd you figure?"

He shrugged. "Not hard to figure out. What happened if you don't mind my asking?"

Willa took a deep breath, preparing herself. "Do you want the long or short version?"

He wanted the long version; there was no doubt about that. He made a show of looking at his watch, making her laugh. "We've got about thirty-five minutes. The long version would pass the time." And give him the needed information to *possibly* hunt the idiot down who put that look on her beautiful face.

"Long version. Okay," she nodded twice, taking another drink, her hand shook a little, and Declan found himself placing a gentle hand on her free one, in comfort and he supposed support. "My ex, Cooper, and I had been together for four years. High school sweethearts, I guess you could say. We met my freshman year, his sophomore year of high school, but didn't run in the same circles. Junior year, we were partnered together in Spanish class and hit it off. We were about a month into the semester when he finally asked me to be his girlfriend." A faint smile played on her lips. "We were inseparable. My entire family loved him. If we vacationed, he was there. And it was the same for his family. He graduated, goes off to SCU. When I graduated the following spring, I didn't know what I wanted to do with my life and didn't want to go into tremendous debt trying to figure it out, so I decided to go to the local community college."

"Smart." He commented. He had done the same thing; no shame in that.

She smiled. "I thought so. We lived only an hour from one another, so it wasn't really that big of a deal. We had even moved into an apartment that was halfway between my friends," she glanced toward a couple dancing, whom he assumed were her friends. "Were dating too, so we made it a whole thing. All four of us in one apartment. They were both attending SCU, as well. So, it made sense. Things were going great, and then I decided that I didn't want to do the college thing anymore. It's not for everyone, so why try to force it? I stuck with it for two semesters before I called it quits." When she paused to take another drink, he held up two fingers to the bartender when he looked their way. The man nodded in acknowledgment as Declan finished off the whiskey.

"So, I quit college, picked up more hours at work. After about six months, I felt this…urge to join the military. On a whim, I went to a recruiter's office. The one I went to had an office for each branch. I didn't know what route to go. All but one of the doors were closed, so I knocked on the door jam and found a recruiter. Turns out he was for the Air Force. All of the other recruiters had gone out to lunch together, but he stayed back because one needed to be there during business hours."

"Lucky him," Declan said. A waitress dropped off their new drinks and took the empty glasses. "Thank you." She nodded and walked away.

"You didn't have to get me another one," Willa said, looking at it.

"Don't worry about it. My treat." Declan smiled at her. "So, you joined the Air Force?"

She nodded. "I did. I work in personnel before you ask." He chuckled, knowing the question was on his mind. "But we're trying a tactic where they send someone out to shadow once a month, and I was given the task. It's really just to make sure that deployed spouses are taken care of, and that there's nothing… unethical happening in the workplace. There's not a point to it, but usually, it's not too bad."

"That doesn't sound like a bad setup." She seemed to enjoy it at least from the soft, wispy look in her eyes, as she spoke.

"It's not. So, back to the long story. Wait, what's the time?" He checked his watch. "We have just over twenty minutes."

"Thank you. So, I joined the Air Force. Cooper was ecstatic; he seemed just as thrilled about this decision as I was. Sofia and Cruz, my friends over there," she pointed to the woman in a sparkly green dress swaying with the man in grey. "Weren't as excited. Sofia and I have been inseparable since we were in diapers, so I understood why. Cooper and I talked about how the future was going to pan out. We wanted to get married, build a life together. We figured we would keep it long distance while he finished college, then once he graduated, he'd get a job wherever I was stationed and could move out of the dorms, and we'd move on with our lives."

Not a bad plan. He could understand how it would be workable, but didn't say anything. By the sound of her voice, she was close to the heartbreak of the story.

"I get stationed here; things were going great. Cruz graduated a semester early and got a job here, at Beta Systems."

When she paused, he took the opportunity to show

he was listening. "I've heard of them. They're a great company."

Willa smiled. "They are. He loves it, and because of this job, I get to have my two closest friends with me. Makes me feel less alone. Anyway. I couldn't move out of the dorm yet, so Cooper decided to stay put for the time being, and we'd just travel back and forth visiting." She paused, taking in a shaky breath. Tears welled in her eyes as she tried blinking them away. Without thinking, he reached for her hand and held it tightly.

"You don't have to tell me. I can see how painful it is for you."

She nodded but continued. "He was supposed to come visit for Valentine's Day weekend. According to Cruz, he had been planning on popping the question. But when the time came, I was at the airport waiting for him, when he called, telling me he never got on the plane." She gripped his hand tighter. "He said he couldn't do the long-distance relationship anymore. He wanted someone who wasn't going to upend his life every few years. Can you believe it? The man who was just as excited about this career path as I had been was now telling me he couldn't handle it. The breakup devastated me. It's been ten months, and I'm *just* now recovering from it. I'm just now able to talk about him without crying. And I go to bed four days a week without crying myself to sleep."

On instinct, he reached a hand to her cheek and wiped away the tear that fell. He couldn't stand the thought that she'd cry over someone so unworthy of her tears. He hated seeing women cry in general, but seeing Willa cry broke something in him.

"I couldn't imagine how that had to have felt. And over Valentine's Day weekend? That's low." He had done some shit things in his life before, but to do that to a woman? Especially one that he had promised so much to? Declan wanted to get on a plane himself and beat the fucker senseless for doing that to her.

Willa let out a weak laugh. "It was. I'm sure it's going to be a tender holiday for me for some time, unfortunately." She sighed. Looked at the dance floor where her friends were oblivious to Willa.

He downed the whiskey, hissing at the burn as it slid down his throat before standing, holding out a hand to her. "Come on, let's dance."

She laughed and shook her head as the song changed to "Perfect". "Do you really want to dance to One Direction?"

Declan shrugged. He had sisters and had spent a few years listening to them being blared on the radio. "We'll make it work. Come on. I need to distract you. No tears in the new year." Checking his watch, he noted they had about five minutes before the countdown. "Will you dance with me, Willa?"

She glanced at his hand before her gaze shifted back to him, taking his hand. The touch sent a shock through him, and he grinned, trying to take her mind off all she had laid bare.

He walked her to the dance floor and pulled her into his arms as they began swaying to the music. She fit perfectly in his arms like she was made to be there. He would gladly dance through *One Direction's* entire catalog if it meant she would always be there.

She dropped her head on his chest, the top of her head reaching his shoulder. Her scent filled his nose, sending want through him. He felt her sigh as she relaxed into him, and he tightened his hold just a little. Declan rested his chin on her head, enjoying the moment while he could, willing time to stop. He may have only known her for under an hour, but it felt like they'd known each other for years. Was that the whiskey talking? Possibly. But he didn't care. Willa felt right, and his heart picked up a little.

When the song ended, they slowed before stopping completely. He felt her shiver from the lack of heat, the large heaters not quite reaching them on the dance floor. He slipped off his jacket and wrapped it around her shoulders. Her green eyes met his as she whispered, "Thank you." He leaned in just a little closer, his eyes flicking down to her lips for a moment.

"Okay, everyone! We have sixty seconds left! Grab a drink and a loved one and get ready to welcome the new year!" A man said from a small makeshift stage, drawing both their attention and easing the growing tension. Willa shifted her body towards him, whether intentional or not, he wasn't sure.

She turned her head towards him, her arms gripping the inside of the jacket to keep it from sliding off her shoulders. He inched a little closer. Declan liked seeing it on her, liked knowing her scent was going to haunt his dreams anytime he wore it now; it was suddenly his favorite item of clothing, besides that maroon dress. "I—I don't want to make you stand here with me, while everyone is celebrating."

He laughed, not meaning to. "Oh no, I want to be

here with you." Declan reached out to grip her chin softly. "You, my dear Willa, need to welcome the new year with someone whom you can rely on." She stared at him, taking in his words, and he knew as the emeralds heated a little that he meant every damn word, as he dropped his fingers from her chin.

The countdown started. This time it felt more, more than just a countdown to a new year, as he watched her, the rest of the world melting away.

Ten.

Nine.

"I barely know you." She whispered, her words suddenly husky, seductive, and every muscle in him tightened at the sound.

Seven.

"I think this is the start of something beautiful." She shifted again, barely an inch closer, both drawn into the others' orbit.

Three.

Two.

One.

Declan closed the gap between them in a millisecond before the crowd burst into a chorus of "Happy New Year!" Her scent enveloped him as he pulled her to him by the lapels of his suit jacket, making her gasp. He smirked as her dark green eyes widened as he pressed his lips against her soft, warm lips.

The moment was electric; time seemed to stand still as he relished the sweetness that was Willa. Her hands found his waist; pressing herself closer, holding onto his shirt tightly as she lost herself in the kiss. His heart was pounding now, as she matched his passion. He felt his knees weaken at the sensation, at the feel of her body pressed against him.

Fireworks exploded above them, into the clear night sky, as his world changed forever.

WILLA WAS LOST in the moment. Declan's lips covered hers gently, but she wanted more, *needed* more. Her body hadn't felt this way in years, not even Cooper affected her this way.

The kiss seemed to last forever, but not long enough at the same time. Her body melted into his, her fingers dug into his sides as the kiss flooded her with emotions, she thought she would never feel again.

Declan pulled back; his blue eyes darkened. Her legs trembled. It was apparent he was feeling the same way as she was. Her heart pounded.

Am I even ready to feel this way about someone?

As if he could read her mind, he kissed her again, quickly. "I like you, Willa. But I don't want to push you into something you're clearly not ready for." He released a breath. "I'm making this decision, so in seven years from now, I can't be mad at myself for this—for friend-zoning myself. If you'll have me. I just don't think I can go through life without you."

She smiled at him, tears forming in her eyes.

This gorgeous man was willing to slide himself into being only friends. How could she refuse?

"I think I'd like that very much."

Chapter Three

"TELL ME AGAIN. What are you doing?" Sofia asked.

Willa sighed into the phone as she stopped in front of Sizzle and Syrup. "I told you. I'm grabbing breakfast with Declan. The guy I met last night."

"I thought you weren't looking for a relationship." She wasn't, but there was something about Declan that made her need to know him better. There was a pull towards him—she felt ridiculous at the thought, but it was undeniable.

"Don't even go there," Willa scoffed, as she leaned against the brick storefront. "He was a really nice guy, and he wants to be friends. *I* want to be friends with him."

"You don't know him," Sofia argued.

Willa rolled her shoulders. "I don't. But that's why I want to do this, Sof. I need someone in my life who doesn't know me the way you do. Someone who hasn't been through all of the shit I've been through like you have. I need this."

Her friend stayed silent so long that Willa checked the phone to make sure the call didn't get disconnected. "Sof?"

"I'm here," another pause. "Just do me a favor and turn on your location. You can't be too careful these days."

"I will, if it's just for your peace of mind, okay?" She took a steadying breath. She knew Sofia was just looking out for her after everything that had happened with Cooper.

"Thank you." Sofia sighed. "Go enjoy your breakfast, and I expect a full report later today."

It was then that Willa saw Declan. Her heart raced with anticipation as he closed the distance. He walked with a confident gait; his hands tucked into the pockets of his brown leather jacket. The early sunlight shone on his face, highlighting his features. She didn't think the lighting last night was terrible, but seeing him now showed her that they definitely dampened his appearance.

She couldn't help but admire the way he carried himself. His tall frame moved gracefully, almost as if he were gliding across the pavement. The way his jacket hugged his broad shoulders and emphasized his muscular build made her heart skip a beat.

Willa hadn't felt this alive in months.

As he drew closer, she could see the smile playing on his lips, and she couldn't help but return it with one of her own. She admired the way his hair tousled in the breeze, the way his smile lit up his face.

"Willa?" Sofia's voice snapped her back to reality.

"What?" She blinked, trying to remember the conversation she was having.

"Full report."

"Oh yeah," she felt a rush of emotion flood through

her as Declan stopped in front of her, his scent wrapping around her. "You got it." She hung up and slid her phone in her pocket.

"Hi." He said when she looked back up at him.

"I was worried you wouldn't come." She admitted, pushing herself off the wall.

"I'm a man of my word." Declan stepped towards the door and pulled it open. "Shall we?"

INSIDE, THEY ORDERED their food before they settled into easy conversation that surprised Willa, as if they had been friends for years.

"So, what do you do for a living?" She asked as their food was dropped off.

"I'm combat control." He answered before taking a bite of his chocolate chip pancakes. A spark of recognition at his words had her leaning just a little closer, another Airman, one who would get it. It made her decide she had made the right choice to give this new friendship a chance.

"I didn't realize you were in the Air Force too."

He nodded as he took a drink of his water. "I didn't know what I wanted to do with my life, so I joined fresh out of high school with a cousin."

"How long has that been?"

"Closing in on five years. I'm twenty-three, by the way." He smiled at her.

A smile tugged at her lips. *Important question number one out of the way.* "I'm twenty-two."

"Glad we got that out of the way." He said with an

answering grin, before taking another bite of his food. She said nothing as she took the first bite of her pancakes.

They ate in comfortable silence, questions plaguing her mind. She felt the need to know anything and everything there was about him, but didn't know where to begin.

Thoughts swirled in her mind about how this was going to be a one-and-done meal, and their *friendship* would end as soon as they walked out the door. Willa let out a sigh of relief when he broke the silence as they finished their meal.

"Siblings?" He asked.

"None." She smiled weakly at him. "My uh—my mom left my dad when I was a baby. Said she couldn't handle being a parent, so she left. It's just been the two of us."

Declan reached across the table to squeeze her hand. "I'm sorry to hear that."

She shrugged. "I've never known any different. Sofia—my friend from last night—is as close to a sibling as I've ever had."

"Are you close with your dad?"

Willa chewed on her lip. How would she answer that? "Yes and no. He's a great parent, don't get me wrong. But he's very…" she trailed off. "Proper? Unaffectionate? I didn't grow up wanting things and was unable to get them. He was very hands-on, just not the kind of parent some kids dream of having."

"He did what he felt was right, I assume."

"Yep." She said, letting the *p* pop as she shifted in

the booth. "What about you? What was Declan Hawke's childhood life like?"

The sudden smile that spread across his face had her breath catching—the look alone told her how close to his family he was. A smile spread across her own face, knowing whatever he said next would be full of love for his family. She envied that. "Well. I grew up in a small town in Utah. A town that the Hawke family has terrorized for decades," he smirked at that, and Willa knew Declan fell into the terrorized the town category of his siblings, "I'm very close to my parents. We Face-Time weekly, phone calls throughout the week if there's something of importance that can't wait, *or,* Heaven forbid, my mom can't reach one of my siblings. I have two brothers and two sisters—"

"Hold on." She leaned forward. "You have four siblings?" She knew the envy shown in her expression. She only ever wanted one to grow up with, but to have so many?

"I do. My oldest brother, Dempsey, is a teacher at the high school we attended not so long ago. Delaney and Taelyn are the twins. Del is training at our local fire and rescue academy. Tae is knee-deep in working on her bachelor's degree. Then the baby is Talia. The wild spirit of the family, who is currently serving her sentence in ninth grade."

"That's a wide variety." She really had no words. "Are you close to them all?"

"I am. We all are, actually. We get together a few times a year when we can manage. Talia has a freaking cell phone already just because she was jealous that she couldn't be a part of the family group chats." Declan's face glowed with laughter.

"I'm going to be honest. I'm insanely jealous that you get to have that privilege."

"If you stick around long enough, I can almost guarantee you'll be added to a chat, too. Then you'll have five Hawke's that don't know how to give you space."

She flashed him a smile. "I think I'd enjoy that. Especially if it means harping on you." Willa tossed a small packet of jelly at him playfully; she loved that she felt so relaxed with him. That her playful side could come out and not feel like she would be judged for it, Cooper would always get annoyed that it was rude or that she was such a child.

Declan slammed a hand to his chest, hurt flicked across his face. "I'm appalled."

Arching an eyebrow, Willa crossed her arms. "I feel like if any of the Hawke siblings likes to cause trouble, it's you."

"It's actually Del, but I'm a close second." He winked at her as their waitress approached, dropping off the check. Without looking, Declan pulled his wallet out, handing a card to the elderly woman. "Thanks."

When she walked away, Willa spoke. "You didn't have to pay for me. I'll pay you back."

"Nonsense. There's a rule in my life when it comes to friends. You don't keep tabs on who pays for what. You can get it next time."

Chapter *Four*

Six Months Later

DECLAN SAT AT his table, unable to tear his gaze away from Willa. He knew where she was, could feel her presence if she were close enough to him. She pulled him into her orbit, one he gladly kept himself near.

The soft shade of blush pink she wore complemented her tanned skin, bringing out the sparkle in her eyes. Her hair was elegantly styled, cascading down her shoulders in soft waves, and her smile was radiant as she chatted with Isabella, Sofia's grandmother.

They had been friends for half a year now, growing closer every day. But seeing her all dressed up today, a wave of emotion washed over him. The feeling wasn't new if he were being honest with himself. He tried pushing the feelings down, but they rose to the surface like a gnawing need. The answer to a question he didn't even know he asked.

He knew, watching her stand beside her best friend, that he was completely and utterly in love with her.

It didn't surprise him; he knew that's where he was going to end up. The way he had cared for her from day one was a dead giveaway, but what he hadn't expected was the rush that filled him when he came to the realization.

When she laughed, he felt himself getting up from his seat and walking towards her.

Her eyes glistened with happiness as they locked on him, making his heart ache with longing.

He knew he was in for a world of trouble if he wasn't careful. But, in that moment, as she looked up at him, those full lips pulled into a smile; he didn't care, just knew he needed to feel her against him in some way. To maybe pretend this could be their moment.

"Ladies," he said as he stopped in front of them, both sets of eyes locked on his. He looked at the older woman. She wore a navy blue lace dress that was both elegant and classic, with intricate detailing that highlighted her timeless style. In classic grandmother fashion, she accessorized with a delicate pearl necklace and matching earrings. "Isabella, when are you going to finally cut me a break and run away with me?"

She blushed, patting at her hair that was pulled back in a classic updo. "Such a charmer, aren't you, Declan?"

He grabbed her hand and pressed a kiss to her knuckles. "Only for you, my dear."

"Oh, stop." She said, dropping her hand. "When are *you* going to finally court this pretty little thing?" *Now, if she would let me.*

Declan followed Isabella's gaze to Willa, whose face had turned the most gorgeous shade of red.

"She simply won't let me, I'm afraid. But I haven't given up yet."

Willa rolled her eyes. "You haven't wooed me enough, I'm afraid."

Isabella looked at Declan again. "Better get on it, young man. She won't be single forever."

No, no, she won't, he thought. She had finally moved past the breakup from Cooper only a few weeks ago, and he wasn't about to rush her into a relationship. "Let's start with a dance," He held a hand up to Willa, waited for her to take it. "Shall we?"

She turned and smiled at Isabella. "We'll finish catching up later?"

"Oh, child," the elderly woman tsked. "Go enjoy your evening."

Before Willa could respond, Declan was already pulling her to the dance floor. He wrapped his arm around her waist, guiding one of her hands to his shoulder as he pulled her into a dance.

Her eyes danced with excitement, and love locked with his.

Declan felt a rush of butterflies in his stomach, his heart stammering in his chest. He wasn't sure if it was excitement or nerves.

They didn't speak, simply swayed to the music, lost in the moment, their eyes locked. Six months in, he couldn't believe how perfectly they fit together, how he could see a future with this woman, even though he was too scared to make any moves. If Parker were here with them, he'd be harping on him to stop being a pussy.

"It was a beautiful ceremony, wasn't it?' She asked, breaking him from his thoughts.

"It was. Perfect for them. I'm glad I was able to come. Even if I was a pity invite." He joked.

She threw her head back in laughter. "They both love you."

"But they pity the soul who attached himself to you."

"Maybe a little pity, but I wouldn't have it any other way." A wicked gleam flicked in her eyes. "It is a shame I've come to love you so quickly, *Cazzo Piccolo*." The Italian flew out of her mouth without hesitation. He loved that she let her guard down so easily around him.

He felt the growl rise in his throat as he pulled her closer and heard the small gasp escape her full lips. "Watch it, la mia dolce figa. You're playing with fire."

Her eyes darkened. "How would you know it's sweet? You've never gotten the chance to find out."

"If you aren't careful, I'm going to find out. I'll find a private room right now and find out."

She arched an eyebrow at him. "Oh yeah? Tell me what you'd do."

He tightened his grip on her waist, leaned in to brush his lips against her ear, and felt her shudder. The smell of her lavender and amber perfume overwhelmed his senses, leaving him dizzy with longing. "If I had you alone, I would make you forget all about your inhibitions. I would touch you in ways that would make you moan with pleasure. Have you begging for more."

He heard her breath hitch as his voice grew husky with desire. "I'd rip this dress off, find out what you're wearing underneath. Bury my face in your pussy and worship you as if you were my final meal."

"Dec," she practically moaned in his ear. He craved that sound, wanted to hear it again while he buried himself in her. His cock hardened slightly at the thought,

He smiled, as vivid images flashed in his mind,

picturing Willa in his arms, succumbing to his every whim, losing herself in the fiery passion that would ignite between them. "I wouldn't stop until I know you've forgotten how to breathe. Until you're begging me for more. Begging me to bury my cock in you and show you how a real man treats his woman."

She gasped. "Declan."

He needed to stop talking before he said fuck it and dragged her off to a room to show her just what he wanted to do to her. Instead, he held himself together, staying the friend she needed, despite how desperately he needed her. He lowered his hand, resting it just at the curve of her ass. "Did I tell you that you look ravishing tonight?"

WILLA'S HEART POUNDED in her chest, long after their dance ended. She couldn't believe the words that had come out of Declan's mouth. Sure, he'd make comments about kissing her, on occasion, actually did, but this time—this time was different.

She knew he was attracted to her. He made it pretty damn obvious, and she knew she wasn't much better. But every word that came out of his mouth sent shivers down her spine. It took everything in her not to drag him off and make him put his mouth on her, bringing his words to life.

When the reception ended, he drove her home, the silence between them heavy. She knew that all she had to do was say the word, and she'd be worshipped in the way he claimed. Would that be so wrong, though? She wanted him, knew he wanted her. But was sex worth the possibility of tomorrow? The risk that they could end their friendship, and she would no longer have him in her life.

"Stop thinking about it, love."

His words had her looking over at him as he parked his car.

"Nothing has to happen." He cupped her chin, turning her head towards him. His blue eyes, serious. "I cherish you, our friendship, way more than a what-if night. I'd love nothing more than to take you upstairs, but I'm not going to rush you. I'll wait forever for you."

Her insecurities began to spiral as she heard Cooper's exact words coming into mind. He promised to many times that he would wait for her, and look where that got her. The thought of opening herself up to that possibility so soon felt too daunting.

"What if I'm never ready?" She asked, her voice barely above a whisper. She reminded herself that her doubts were amplified from the high of the wedding, of seeing her best friends in love. Declan didn't expect anything more from her—not really.

"I'll wait for you, Willa. I always will." She nodded, wanting to believe it. He opened his mouth to say something, but stopped when his phone went off. "Sorry, hold on."

He pulled his phone out and slid his finger across the screen. “Hey, Mom. What’s up?”

Willa sighed a breath of relief. She wanted this conversation to be over. To not think about what could be between them.

“You’re in town?” A pause. “I’m off tomorrow, I can come by and see you.”

His eyes slid to Willa’s. “Yeah, she has tomorrow off too. She’s driving them to the airport for their honeymoon.”

Willa started to fidget with the soft fabric of her dress. She knew what was coming.

“I’m sure she’ll love to meet you. Lunch then?” He nodded as he listened. “Okay. We’ll see you then. Text me the address.”

He hung up the phone and dropped it in the cup holder. “Well, Miss Evans. You’re going to meet my parents tomorrow.”

Oh boy.

Chapter *Five*

"I'M SORRY THIS isn't what you need to be listening to today," Willa said as she parked her car outside of Terminal B, chewing on her bottom lip. She was so nervous about meeting Declan's parents; she had a feeling she was going to wear a hole in her lip.

"Uh, no. Do not be sorry," Sofia said, unbuckling herself. "I'm sorry that we're leaving today, and I don't get a full rundown until after we get back."

Willa groaned as she got out of the car. "I'm sure you'll have a few dozen texts when you land." She shook her head. "I don't know why I'm so nervous to meet them."

Cruz shut the trunk with a laugh. "It's because you're madly in love with him already, and they're going to be your in-laws someday."

She rolled her eyes. "Just because you are both happily in love and in your own bubble doesn't mean it's going to happen to me. We're *just* friends."

Mischief flashed across Sofia's face before she was pulled in for a hug. "I said the same thing once upon a time. Now look at me."

She did. Her best friend glowed—she was happy, in

love, and starting her life with her husband. "Yeah, yeah. You guys better go."

"We'll see you in a week, okay? Send updates." Sofia said, pulling her into another hug. Willa squeezed her friend as she felt the tears welling.

Don't cry. "I won't spare a detail." She pulled Cruz in for a quick hug before she turned to get back in her car. With a quick wave, she buckled in and headed to Declan's apartment.

"I STILL DON'T know why you expect me to go hiking," Willa groaned, climbing out of Declan's car. She felt herself shaking as she shut the door. The nerves that settled in her stomach were making her feel a little nauseous. She took a deep, steadying breath—the crisp summer air filling her lungs.

"Because fresh air is good for you and it's something that my family has always done," Declan answered, grabbing their duffel bags from the backseat. Willa tried arguing that she wouldn't need a change of clothes, but listened when he kept insisting.

"I don't hike, Dec. I will probably fall and get hurt."

"You'll be fine." He laughed as she sent him a pointed look. "I'll be with you."

"And what if I fall and get hurt? I'm a crybaby when I get hurt. I don't want to risk embarrassment." *Please let me avoid this.*

He rolled his eyes as he walked around the car. "Stop trying to get out of it. You'll have two strong men to keep you from getting hurt."

Declan put his hands on her shoulders and squeezed. "You're going to be fine, Willa. This is just a casual get-together with my parents. They're the most laid-back people I've ever met."

She shot him a look. "Easy for you to say, because you've known them your entire life. You didn't have to worry about making a good first impression."

He laughed, throwing an arm around her shoulder, before guiding her towards the cabin. She fought the urge to nuzzle into him as they walked. He smelled damn good.

Willa focused on the world around them to take her mind off her nerves. The sun cast a warm golden hue, shining gently through the trees. With each step taking her closer to the cabin, she studied the structure that appeared as though it had sprouted from the earth itself. Its beams were sturdy, dark, and weathered.

She felt the sensation of anticipation bubble as Declan knocked on the door.

Why *was* she so nervous? She had no reason to be so worked up about meeting Declan's parents. They had to be wonderful—the man Declan was, reflected that. *Right?*

As the door swung open, Willa struggled to stifle the gasp that rose in her throat.

Connor Hawke was Declan in twenty-five years—there was no question about that. The gray hair at his temples and hazel eyes were the only things that made him stand out from his son. As he pulled his son in a warm embrace, his face was radiant with joy. Willa was surprised by the pang of envy that hit her.

"Hey, Dad, it's good to see you," Dec said, patting his dad on the back.

"You too, son." His eyes slid over. "You must be Willa."

She smiled as he pulled her in for a hug as well. His scent of cardamom and white cedar wrapped around her. She felt herself relax in his arms—this kind of open affection wasn't something she was used to.

"It's so nice to meet you," she trailed off. *Shit.* What was she supposed to call him?

"Connor, please. Declan has told us so much about you, I feel like you're already family. Come in." He stepped aside, letting them enter.

As Willa stepped inside, she couldn't help but think that there was something special—and a little corny—about log cabins.

The right side of the cabin opened into a living area that beautifully mirrored the serene landscape outside. The walls, constructed from the same robust logs as the exterior, created a seamless transition, making it feel as if she were still outside but sheltered from the elements. The room exuded a cozy warmth, enveloping her in comfort. Rich green leather furniture echoed the shades of pine needles and moss outside, enhancing the tranquil ambiance.

She found the atmosphere to be deeply calming and could appreciate that.

"Ahh, you're here!" A woman's voice came from Willa's left. She turned to find Norah standing in the kitchen.

Norah Hawke was every bit as captivating as her husband. Her blonde hair was elegantly swept back into a ponytail, and her blue eyes sparkled with excitement.

A smile spread across Willa's face as Norah made her way around the kitchen island and wrapped her in a hug. When they separated, Norah held onto her hands. "I've been so excited to meet you. I feel like I already know you."

"I feel the same," Willa said. "Truly. Declan speaks so highly of both of you."

Norah beamed; a mother proud of her son. Envy crept into Willa's stomach; the want for a mother sent a pang through her heart. She loved her dad, but sometimes a girl just needs her mom, and this woman in front of her was everything she could have wanted in a mother.

"Declan says you love sweet tea, right?"

"Y-yes." Willa could feel the slight blush warming her cheeks, that Declan had mentioned something as trivial as her preferred drink. If she wasn't careful, she would give in to what Cruz had joked about earlier. *Love.*

Norah kept one of Willa's hands in her own as she led her back to the kitchen. "I made sure to buy some tea bags and sugar when we got in last night. I wanted to make sure you were comfortable here."

"Oh." What was she supposed to say to that? She wasn't used to people going out of their way for her like that. "You didn't have to."

"Nonsense. It's the least we could do." She poured four glasses of tea, handing them out. She took a drink before she continued. "Now, I want to know all about you."

. . .

DECLAN FELT AT home in the mountains, regardless of which range it was. He loved how vastly different the Appalachians were from the Rocky Mountains.

The fresh, crisp mountain air had a unique way of filling his lungs, seeming to always pull him into a new mindset. It felt as though he could shed the burdens of his everyday life and give in to the wild side—the side that craved the symphony of nature, where the whispers of the wind told their own stories. Every time he came to the mountains, he yearned to feel the damp, soft soil beneath his toes and the bite of rock against his feet; there was a reminder that he was a guest in nature's domain, not the other way around.

Twenty-three years on this earth, and he never tired of it.

He took in his surroundings as he hiked the winding trails—the towering trees, their trunks thick and gnarled with age, stood sentinel on either side, their emerald canopies filtering the sunlight into a kaleidoscope of soft greens and golds.

Declan took the time to study Willa, the way she looked at his mom when they chatted. A smile spread across his face, thinking about how nervous she was just a few hours ago. He knew his parents would make her feel welcome as if she had been a member of their family her entire life.

He knew that's what she needed. Someone like Willa thrived the most when she was around people she knew and loved. He knew she hated the awkward phases of meeting someone and getting to know them, and was thankful that she relaxed around him almost immediately. It felt, even to him, that they had known one another for a lot longer than six months.

Watching Willa now with his mom, you wouldn't have known they had met only mere hours ago.

Connor, who had been leading them, pulled back, waiting for Declan, allowing Willa and Norah to continue their conversation.

"I'm glad we got the chance to meet her. I can see why you've talked about her so much."

Declan slid his eyes from Willa to his dad. "I haven't talked about her *that* much." *Dad was exaggerating.*

Connor let out a laugh, causing both women to look over their shoulders at him. He waved them off. "Son, you've talked about her more than Talia talks about Michael B. Jordan."

Declan scrunched his nose. "Please do not compare me to my teenage sister."

He knew all about Talia and her obsession with the actor and knew there was no way in hell he had talked about Willa *that* much.

Fuck. *Had* he been talking about her that much?

Without thinking, he pulled his phone out of his pocket and opened up the message chain labeled, *Look What the Stork Dragged In*.

DEC

I don't need shit for this right now, but how often do I talk about Willa?

He didn't have to wait long for a response.

DEL

As annoying as Talia is with her MBJ bullshit.

"There's no way I'm that bad," Declan muttered as he read the conversation.

DEC

Seriously?

TAELYN

So annoying Dec.

Don't get me wrong, I'm sure we'll all love her, but you are definitely lovesick.

DEL

It's so gross.

He heard his dad chuckle. Glancing over, he caught him reading the messages as they came in.

TAELYN

Don't even talk about gross, Mr. third wheel.

Declan rolled his eyes when Delaney's response was a middle finger emoji.

DEMPSEY

Let me know when the wedding is, little bro.

Shoving his phone back in his pocket, he said. "I really am that bad."

"Oh shit!" Willa yelled.

Declan looked up to watch her fall to the ground. "Fuck." He jogged up to where she and his mom were. "Are you okay?"

She looked from him to his parents, her cheeks tinted pink from embarrassment. He tried to keep a straight face, but the smile slipped through. He knew she liked to keep her language polite—a habit from her upbringing.

"I tripped over that root," she pointed, guiding his attention to a large tree root sticking out of the ground. "And I think I hurt my ankle."

He reached for her right foot. 'I'm going to check, okay?"

She nodded, giving him the permission he needed.

Declan slipped off her shoe and pulled her sock off. He had been around his fair share of broken ankles and felt he could confidently say hers was only sprained. "Let's try to get you on your feet. If we need to go to the hospital, I think there's one a few miles away."

"It's about three miles west," Norah confirmed.

He looked into Willa's eyes, saw the worry in them. He cupped her cheeks. "Hey, you'll be fine, okay."

She nodded, then said, "I told you I was going to get hurt."

Declan smiled, unable to help himself. "I think you did it on purpose. Come on, let's get up."

He stood, pulling her up with him carefully. She took a deep breath before hesitantly putting her foot on the ground. Willa took a small step, then another.

"How does it feel?" Norah asked.

"Feels okay. I can walk at least, but I don't know if I can make it back to the cabin." She looked at Norah. "How far is the cabin?"

Declan turned to his mom, who was tapping away on her phone. "We're just shy of 5 miles out."

Willa groaned. "What are we going to do? I don't think I can walk three miles, let alone five."

He smirked at her as he scooped her into his arms. "Dec! Put me down!"

"Sorry, love. It's gotta be done."

Love. Declan felt his heart start to pound in his chest at the word.

"Dec," she complained. "It took us two hours to make it this far. You can't possibly carry me that long."

He turned and started making his way down the trail that they had already walked. "I will do it because we need to get you back to the cabin. Now stop fucking arguing with me."

Declan watched her open and shut her mouth, defeated. *Good.*

LITTLE OVER two hours later, Norah led Declan to the second bedroom of their cabin.

"I'm sure this comes as no surprise, Dec,

but I'm going to insist you two stay the night. You have to be exhausted."

He was. Carrying Willa wasn't a big deal, and he felt pretty good being able to help her when she needed it. But he'd be lying if he didn't say he was worn out. Between the wedding yesterday and the four hours of hiking—he knew if his head hit the pillow right now, he'd be asleep in under a minute.

"Thanks, Mom." Declan sat Willa down after Norah pulled the blankets down, as Connor came in with two extra pillows to prop Willa's ankle on.

"I'm so sorry," Willa said, shifting on the bed to get comfortable. "I told Declan when we got here, it was going to be a bad idea if I went hiking."

"Nonsense," Norah said. "It happens all the time."

"You're on a trip. You shouldn't have to cut your time short because I got hurt. I really am sorry."

"We raised five children. Three of whom are boys. I can confidently say that we've been there, done that." Connor laughed, nodding in agreement. "Don't feel sorry. I'm going to get you some ice for that ankle."

"And I think I'm going to order a pizza. I'm starving."

Declan watched his parents leave the room before he kicked off his shoes. "Is there a bath or shower I can use?" She asked. "I know you did all the hard work coming back, but I feel absolutely disgusting."

He stood and walked over to check for an attached bathroom—finding it on the first try. "Right here. Soaker tub or shower with a bench?"

"Mmm, tub please," Willa moaned. Declan's cock jolting at the sound. What he'd give to make her moan like that on a regular basis. "I think a bath and pizza sounds perfect."

"Aren't you glad I made you bring extra clothes?" He asked, cocking an eyebrow.

She rolled her eyes. "If I knew getting to take a hot bath was in the cards, I would've packed better."

Declan grabbed his duffel bag and stepped into the bathroom, and turned on the water. He found a small bag of Epsom salt under the sink and poured half of its contents into the tub.

He hopped in the shower as the tub filled, needing to rinse off the sweat from the day.

After quickly drying off, he threw on the basketball shorts he packed, opting to skip the shirt. He turned off the water once the tub was full and stepped into the bedroom, where he found Willa fast asleep.

She looked so at peace. He wanted to lie down with her and pull her into his arms while she slept.

He turned when he heard a soft knock, before the door opened, revealing his mom. She smiled softly at him. "I had a feeling she'd fall asleep." She handed him the bag of ice she wrapped in a kitchen towel. "Connor is ordering pizza; we'll save what's left for when she wakes up."

"Thanks again, Mom." Declan said, "I'm sorry this is how our day ended up."

"Like I told her, we raised five of you. This happened a time or two." Norah reached up and ran a hand over his cheek. Without thinking, he leaned into her touch as he always did. "Thank you for letting us meet her. I hope we get to see a lot more of her."

He nodded but said nothing as she left the room.

Walking to the bed, he laid the bag on Willa's ankle. She shifted slightly as the cold touched her skin, but settled back in.

Walking to the left side of the bed, he grabbed the pillow to take out to the living room.

"Dec?" Willa's sleep-heavy voice asked. *Shit*.

He looked at her as she rolled over slightly to pull the blanket over her body.

"Hey, love. I'm here."

"Will you stay with me? I don't want to be alone tonight."

His heart thundered in his chest. Clearing his throat, he managed, "Yeah, of course."

Declan dropped the pillow back on the bed before he pulled the covers back to climb in. "Come here."

He scooted himself to the middle of the bed, pulling her into his arms. He shouldn't be doing this, but there was no way he could resist.

Just this one time, he told himself.

Just once, and fell asleep, with the woman of his dreams wrapped in his arms.

Chapter *Six*

Three Years Ago

"WILLA!" DECLAN CALLED out as he let himself into her apartment, not wanting to be late for Sofia's early birthday dinner. He fidgeted with the hot pink glittery key that had become the bane of his existence once his coworkers caught a glimpse of it, even if it did give him access to come see her whenever he wanted. The day she moved in last year, she handed him the key, along with a fuzzy kitten keychain, and was insistent that he use it in case of emergencies. He begged her for a manlier key, but she laughed and said he took what she gave him, or he didn't get one at all. He grumbled about it but took the damn thing. Even now, he caught himself rubbing his thumb across the kitten's head, smiling to himself.

He tossed the keys into the green ceramic bowl on her kitchen counter, courtesy of his mother, as he went in search of his friend.

The muffled sound of Willa's favorite boy band wafted through the air, telling him she was still in the shower.

He made his way towards her bedroom, the smells of her soaps, lotions, and whatever else she used to unknowingly torture him filled his lungs, setting him on edge. He could never gauge what she would smell like on a week-by-week basis, but whatever was her given favorite this week had him needing her. *Craving* what he couldn't have.

Because like the dumbass that he was, he friend-zoned himself four years ago. He had needed her as much as he needed his next breath, but when she told him what had happened between her and Cooper, he didn't want to be a rebound but knew he couldn't walk out of her life. The proposal of them just being friends was the best decision he had made. He had helped her through the remainder of the depression fog that the asshole had caused after he failed to see what she was worth. Declan had been there for it all over the last four years and held his head high when he watched Willa kick the asshole to the curb when he pathetically tried crawling back to her.

He pushed the bedroom door open; the sound of the shower running barely registered as he took in the ivory dress lying on her dark blue comforter. He could already see how it would end up hugging her every curve, the image causing his mouth to water, feeling himself hardening.

Fuck. He needed to calm down.

As they grew closer in friendship, so did the amount of physical contact. They snuggled during movie nights and idly held hands when they walked around the city together. Countless times he had pulled her into a dance while they cooked together, wanting to get lost in the moment, dreaming of what they could have together. Their time together had been pure bliss, in Declan's mind, but also a lingering hell as he chose to torture himself.

He strolled over to the wall of windows, running parallel to her bed. She had mentioned the breathtaking view was the main reason why she chose this place. She told him she felt like a queen in her castle overlooking her kingdom. As he gazed out the windows now, he understood why. The city below was illuminated with lights, hinting at the possibilities that lay within. He felt like a king himself, looking over his dominion. He longed to stand there with Willa in his arms, taking in the warmth of her body, tracing his hands over her enticing curves, and kissing her neck while savoring the soft moans he knew she would make. He imagined the thrill of sliding into her against these windows, risking the possibility of being seen as she screamed out his name with every thrust.

Declan had been so lost in thought, he hadn't heard her shower turn off. The sound of her singing in attempted harmony cut through the silence.

He smiled to himself as she wailed about being someone's good night, always insisting on being like fucking Snow White, singing every chance she got, and he made sure to harp on her about it at every single opportunity.

He pictured her putting on the dress he had seen on the bed. Watching the fabric slide down her body as she fit it into place.

Wait…

The dress was on the bed. Which only meant—

He turned just in time to see Willa walking out of her bathroom, her soft blue silk robe sliding from her shoulders, pooling at her feet. Exposing her toned, tanned body that was clad in only a lacey white strapless bra, that pushed her breasts up in a way that made his fingers itch to touch. His eyes shamelessly watched as she rubbed her hands over her face in frustration. It wasn't until he watched her hands drop to her hips that he noticed the matching white panties.

Fuck. Me.

He hadn't realized he groaned out loud until her green eyes snapped to his in shock.

"What the fuck, Dec!" she squealed as she slammed a hand to her chest, which just made things worse because it brought his attention to the heavy rise and fall of her breasts. "You scared the shit out of me!"

He arched a brow at her when her hands remained against her chest, and she looked down. He couldn't help but smile as she turned red when she realized she was practically naked in front of him. She quickly grabbed her robe from where it was discarded on the floor.

"I called when I came in." He was still watching her every move, and it filled him with smug satisfaction that he made her this flustered.

"I didn't hear you." Her voice was now soft, as she held the robe against her chest, biting her lip. The image, so innocent and demure, sent blood right down to his half-hardened cock. Why did she have to be so fucking sexy?

Shaking the thought away, he leaned against the wall, crossing his arms, hoping to keep her attention above his waist as he spoke, his voice huskier than he expected. "Not my fault, you never listen."

Willa let out a huff of frustration before moving to her bed and threw one of her decorative pillows at him. He caught it and smiled at her. In her fit of irritation, she had forgotten all about the robe in her hands and was once again, nearly naked before him.

The sight of her chest heaving, her green eyes wild and bright, had him imagining closing the distance between them. Grabbing ahold of her luscious curves, throwing her down on the bed, watching her chestnut hair fall around her, and leaning in to—he closed his eyes, letting out a breath.

Keep it together, Hawke.

They watched each other for a moment, her eyes darkening, as if in challenge.

He made to move toward her. To take that challenge on, when she huffed and grabbed her robe off the floor, *again,* this time sliding it over her shoulders, securing it loosely around her waist.

She walked to her dresser, grabbing the diamond stud earrings he had gifted her for her birthday. The one stipulation Willa had given him was that she didn't like accepting jewelry, but the earrings were the one thing she wore regularly, and he loved that. He felt something possessive in him every time he was with her, and she wore them. Like she was telling the world she was his.

Seeing her now, in nothing but a robe and the earrings, stirred something primal in his gut. Without a word, he pushed off the wall and closed the distance between them, stopping when his chest brushed up against her back.

Willa secured the second earring before bracing her hands on the edge of her dresser. Declan leaned in slightly, inhaling her soap. "Lilac and lemons." He muttered under his breath. The scent was intoxicating, clouding his mind with lust.

"With a hint of amber," her voice came out in a squeak.

"Mmm," he couldn't think. He didn't want to think.

Declan leaned in, his lips lightly brushing the soft skin at the base of her neck. He felt the sharp intake of her breath.

Eyes full of desire, he looked up at her in the mirror as he reached for the top of her robe, sliding it slowly down her shoulder while his finger gently glided along the skin of her collarbone.

"Dec," she whispered, leaning back into him, closing her eyes, as his lips found her skin again.

"Tell me to stop, Willa." He reached for the knot in her robe, held it in his hands, and waited for her answer.

He needed her to make the decision. She needed to tell him to stop, not to cross the line. It surprised him when she dropped her hands to where he held her robe, loosened the knot.

"I'm not going to do that." She answered as her robe slid open, locking eyes with his, her eyes full of need. "I've wanted this for so long, Dec."

"Tell me what you want." He croaked out. Was she really saying what he had been desperate to hear all these years? He braced his hands on the dresser, encasing her.

"You." She turned toward him and allowed the robe to slide off her body, exposing an almost naked body for the third time tonight. "I want to be yours, Declan."

. . .

WILLA GASPED WHEN Declan slammed his lips against hers.

The kiss was full of emotion, passion, *desire*. Her world tilted on its axis as Declan's tongue slid against her lips, demanding entrance. When she opened for him, he took, claiming what had been his for four long years. Igniting like a wildfire, a heated dance of intertwining lips and tongues. The taste that was Declan was intoxicating, the sensation sent shivers down her spine.

He broke the kiss to run his lips down her throat to her collarbone, while his hands found their way to her lace-covered breasts, running his thumbs over her hardened nipples.

"Willa," he growled out when she let out a moan. Her hands busied themselves with his black shirt, fighting with each button. When the final button was undone, she ripped the shirt open, his toned stomach on full display. She dragged her nails down his abs and around his waist as he unfastened her bra, tossing it aside as the cool air hit her breasts. "God, I've wanted to do this for years."

He grabbed her ass, pulling her into his arms as he sat her on her dresser, her breasts directly in his face.

Without a moment's hesitation, he leaned in and pulled a nipple into his hot mouth. Nipped, sucked. Willa buried her hands in his hair, keeping his mouth planted *firmly* on her.

"Oh God, Dec."

He switched breasts, his fingers replacing his mouth. Willa moved her hands to his pants and started working on his belt. She needed the damned thing off of him, *now*. Dec shifted, kicking off his shoes as she pushed his pants and boxers down, his cock springing free. She gasped at his size. She knew he was big, but she wasn't expecting *this.* He let out a hiss as the air hit him. "Now, please."

Declan grabbed her ass again, lifting her from the dresser as he spun them around, tossing her on the bed, her head hitting the pillows. She shifted her upper body to lean on her elbows when he stood at the edge of the bed, watching her.

"Dec?"

His dark eyes met hers with fire blazing in them. "You are absolutely breathtaking, Willa." She felt her cheeks redden. Why the fuck was she embarrassed by that? "Even more when you get all flushed." He kneeled, crawling up the bed between her thighs.

Declan hovered over her, his face mere inches from her, where she knew she was *soaked*.

"Should we play first?" he asked, as he leaned down, brushing his lips along her hip. She squirmed under him. Let out a shallow moan when his teeth scraped.

"Dec—" she moaned again, as he hooked his fingers

on her panties, pulling them down her legs, as slow as humanly possible.

He slid her panties off, discarding them over his shoulder, as he stared at her. He grabbed his cock, pumping it torturously slow. She needed to move. Needed to replace his hand with hers. Needed to know if she could fit all of him in her mouth. When she started to sit up to *assist*, he stopped her.

"My turn first, love." He leaned in, kissing her deeply before he nudged her back against the bed. He positioned his face between her legs and rubbed his nose briefly against her clit, causing her to gasp. "For four long years, I've wanted to know what you tasted like." He flicked his tongue out, dragging it against her center, slowly. "What would you sound like if I did this." He pulled her clit into his mouth, nibbled gently.

"Declan," Willa moaned as pleasure shot through her body, causing her back to arch.

"I've wanted to know how tight you'd feel when I slid my fingers into you." He slid a finger in as his mouth sucked on her clit again. "So, so tight." He pumped his finger into her, curling inside her, hitting that sweet spot. "You will be suffocating when I slide my cock into you."

"Dec. Please." She panted. She needed him to *move*. Finger. Mouth. Something. *Anything.*

"What's the matter, love? Am I not moving fast enough for you?" He looked up at her, his eyes crinkling in the corner, which told her he was smiling.

"You're being torturous. Please. I need you."

His expression darkened, rocking her to her core.

She yelped when he nipped at her inner thigh. "Your wish is my command."

He dropped his head again, sucking her clit into his mouth as he pushed two fingers into her. She cried out in pleasure at the sensation. His tongue followed his teeth, soothing wherever he nipped, before he started the process over again. Declan removed his fingers only to replace them with his tongue, like a starving man at a feast. She felt the pressure building and knew she was right there, on the verge of a mind-blowing orgasm.

He must've sensed it, for he replaced his tongue with his fingers again, pumping and curling into her, as his tongue flicked across her clit once…twice…three times. She was *so close* to falling over the edge in ecstasy when—

The shrill sound of Declan's ringtone started startling both of them.

"You've got to be kidding me." He muttered against her sweaty skin. He looked up at her, his face full of regret from the interruption. "I'm sorry."

He crawled off the bed, leaving her naked on the bed. She sat up and pulled her legs up to her chest. Not out of modesty, but because she felt overly exposed. Only one contact had that ringtone on his phone. It was the same one she had for her commanding officer.

Fuck. That's not good. Declan grabbed his pants and pulled out his phone. "Hawke."

Silence fell as he listened. Willa watched him, standing gloriously naked in her bedroom like he owned the room.

When did they get here? How did they get here?

She didn't know, and honestly, didn't care. Willa had

spent countless nights imagining what life would be like if they were a couple. He had grown accustomed to her need for physical touch when they were together, so he knew something was up if she didn't immediately snuggle up to him. Sure, friends could be that close, but the way they were together? They were a couple without being the actual couple part.

He turned his gaze to her, his eyes full of emotion. She knew that look. Declan hung up the phone and set it on her dresser.

Willa wiped at the tears that spilled over. She didn't want to cry. She *couldn't* cry. Not when it meant he was leaving, and they'd have to say goodbye.

"When do you leave?" she asked, her voice barely a whisper. She was doing everything she could to keep her emotions in check. Deploying was hard enough, but to be weak, to display those feelings for someone else who was deploying, was worse. Declan had more important things to worry about right now.

He bent down to grab his pants, sliding them on before he answered. "Payne said to report at o' five hundred hours." Leaving his pants unbuttoned, he grabbed his shirt and her robe from the floor.

Fuck. They had to meet Cruz and Sofia at The Silent Mirror for dinner soon. That wouldn't give them much, if any, time to talk about what just happened.

She needed to move. If she didn't, she would stay in bed, wallowing in her emotions, probably putting herself back into a depression haze that he wouldn't be here to get her out of.

He slid his shirt on, leaving it unbuttoned as well, his toned body exposed, as if buttoning his clothes shut the door on what had just happened between them.

Willa climbed out of bed and slid her robe on when he handed it to her, securing the band around her waist, before wrapping her arms around herself.

"Hey." He looked at her more closely now. Declan closed the distance between them, pulling her into his arms as the tears spilled over the edge. He pressed his lips to her temple. "Let's go enjoy our night, we'll find time to talk about it."

"I don't want this to ruin their night out."

"We won't let this put a damper on the night."

She nodded. He knew she didn't fully believe him, but it was all he had.

Chapter Seven

WILLA WAS SO lost in her own thoughts during dinner, the only thing that kept her going into a full panic attack was the constant physical contact Declan made. She wondered if what happened between them was obvious to Sofia and Cruz.

She let her thoughts wander at the thought of what could've happened had he not gotten that phone call. She thought about that first kiss, the need that Declan poured into it. Honestly, how was she supposed to *not* think about that?

The fire that blazed in Declan's blue eyes, the way that look alone had her soaking wet.

Even now, she shifted in her seat, crossing her legs to alleviate *some* of the ache. She had never known a man who was so in tune to her body, who knew how to make her feel the way that he did in her bedroom.

Declan laid his hand on her thigh, his fingers pressing into her skin rough enough to jolt her out of her thoughts.

Willa snapped her gaze to him, as her cheeks heated. The look he was giving her told her that he knew exactly where her mind was. In response, his hand crept further along her thigh, sliding inward just a touch as he did so.

She let out a gasp at the pressure of his fingers, causing Cruz to stop talking. Willa looked at Sofia, who smirked with a knowing glance. She smiled back, hoping the smile was enough to keep Sofia from asking what was on her mind.

Willa smiled weakly as their waiter showed up, dropping off the check for Declan to sign.

When Sofia looked back at Cruz as he started talking about something their one-year-old, Holly, did.

She smiled, watching her friends' faces light up at the mention of their daughter. How amazing was it to watch someone you've known for years go through the highs and lows of life, watching them find love and start a family of their own? Willa couldn't wait for that life of her own. She wondered if *maybe*, just maybe, she and Dec could have that.—the family, the deep love.

Looking over at Declan, his eyes were on hers, that same fire from earlier in his eyes.

He leaned in and pressed his lips to the skin just below her ear. "Keep looking at me like that and I will bend you over this table and fuck you in front of everyone."

"Fuck, Declan," she moaned, before realizing where they were and clapped a hand over her mouth. He chuckled in her ear before he pulled back to sign the check.

Willa flushed and looked across the table, where Sofia and Cruz watched her.

"We need to talk," Sofia said to her before she kissed Cruz on the cheek and motioned for Willa to follow.

She sighed and closed her eyes. Standing, she shot Declan a glare before she followed Sofia outside.

"WHEN THE FUCK did you and Declan finally have sex?" Sofia asked, whirling on Willa as soon as she stepped outside.

"Sof. What the fuck," Willa hissed, looking around for anyone who could overhear. Willa tried to pull Sofia off to the side, further away from people entering and leaving the restaurant. Sofia merely shrugged off the hold, her eyes blazing with so many questions.

"No. You're going to tell me, *right now*. I've been dying for you two to finally do it, and the night has finally happened!"

Willa let out a laugh at Sofia's excitement. "We did… things."

"Girl," she dragged out the word. "I love Cruz, and our sex life is still thriving, but come *on*. I need details. Stat."

"Well," she trailed off. What all was she willing to tell now? "He came over to pick me up, and I was still in the shower."

"Ooh, the first time was shower sex?" Sofia begged to know.

"No. We uhm—" She felt tears beginning to prickle, thinking about why they had to stop.

Shit. Fuck. Shit.

Sofia stared at her, waiting for an explanation.

"I—he…" the tear slipped over, falling down her

cheek. She watched as Sofia's expression went from excitement to concern.

Before she knew it, the tears wouldn't stop. She buried her face in her hands as Sofia's arms wrapped around her. She felt Sof pull her off toward where a bunch of bushes lined the walkway of *The Silent Mirror,* away from anyone to hear her cries.

She didn't make it. She told Declan she would keep herself together tonight. She knew she was ruining their night out.

"What the *fuck* did you do?" Sofia hissed.

Willa didn't need to turn around to know she was talking to Declan. *When did he come outside?*

"What do you mean? Willa?" Concern heavy in Declan's voice.

"I was making her spill the details on what happened between the two of you, and she started crying." Sofia's arms tightened around Willa.

Say something, idiot.

"Hold on." Cruz said, "Did you hurt her?" Willa had never heard Cruz speak with such venom in his voice. If she weren't in such despair at the turn of events, she would have gasped at his threatening tone.

"No," came Declan's quick response.

"You better not be fucking lying to me. I swear to God, Declan."

"I would *never* hurt her. Fuck!" Declan yelled. "I got the call right when we were…occupied."

"What call?" Sofia asked, her arms slackening on Willa.

"I'm being deployed. Tomorrow morning."

"What the fuck, Dec?" Sofia hissed. She released Willa. "I'm sorry. I thought—"

"No, don't apologize." He walked to Willa and pulled her into his arms as he pressed a kiss to her head. "You had every right to jump to conclusions."

"I'm sorry, Sof. I've been trying to hold it in all night. We didn't want to tell you guys when we first got here, and it spoil the night."

"Oh, Willa," Sofia's eyes softened.

"What time tomorrow?" Cruz asked.

"Five."

"Shit." Willa watched Sofia's eyes travel to Cruz's phone when he checked the time. "You guys should've told us earlier. You only have seven hours. I'm assuming you need to pack on top of sleeping."

Declan nodded. "Unfortunately."

"Okay, well, let's say goodbye now, so you can get back to your apartment and do what you need to do," Sofia said. "I'll meet you tomorrow morning, okay?" She said to Willa, knowing she was going to be at the airfield to say goodbye.

"No, please—"

"Don't even finish that sentence. I know I have Holly, but Cruz will take morning duty while I meet you there. I know you, and I know you're going to be too worked up to drive home."

"She's right," Declan said. "I wouldn't even have you there if I could help it…"

Willa shot him a look. There was no way in hell she would say goodbye to him.

"But, I'd appreciate it if someone were there to drive you home."

She groaned but nodded, knowing she wasn't going to get her way. "Fine."

DECLAN DROPPED WILLA's bag on his couch before he turned to her. She looked worried, but he could tell she was trying to hide it.

She convinced him to let her stay at his place tonight —not only to help him pack but because she wanted to soak in the time they had left. He knew they needed to talk about it, but it was late, and he just wanted to soak up his time with her.

He headed to his coat closet, where he kept his luggage, pulling out his large green loadout bag and his favored black backpack.

Handing Willa his backpack, to pack chargers, his laptop, and other essentials for the flight, before he headed into his room.

In his closet, he began pulling out uniforms, socks, boxer briefs, and undershirts, methodically gathering everything he needed. He reached for a second pair of boots—a precaution he always took. Growing up, he and his siblings always gave his mom grief for having toiletries pre-packed, but tonight, he was thankful for that habit. He grabbed his bag and dropped it into the bag.

Once he was finished packing, he carried the bag into the living room to place it by the door. A glance at the clock told him it was after one.

He looked at Willa, who was half asleep on the couch, wrapped in a dark orange fuzzy blanket she bought for him last year. He hated the idea of waking her up, knowing they needed to talk about what happened between them—what they needed to be ready for when he returned.

"Willa," he whispered, touching her gently on the shoulder.

Her eyes fluttered open. "Shit, I'm sorry. I finished a while ago and needed a minute."

"It's okay. I only just finished. Do you want to talk or go to bed?"

"What time is it?"

"Just after one."

"I really do want to sleep, but we should talk about what happened."

He sat down on the couch beside her. "Look, I want to, but let's just not."

"Dec—" she started to argue. He understood why, but maybe now wasn't the best time.

"Hold on. Can we put a bookmark on this? Come back to it when I get back?" He grabbed her hand. "I know it's important, but I feel like this is a conversation that deserves our full attention."

"And we're both too wound up thinking about you leaving," She finished.

He nodded. "I'd love to start this between us, but I don't want to finally get the girl, only to leave her behind for six months."

"Okay. Bookmark inserted; book closed." She said, half joking. "For now." He could hear the unaired words; *the minute you get home, this will be the first thing.*

Without thinking, he leaned in and pressed his lips to hers. He poured his heart and soul into this kiss. He wanted her to *feel* how he was feeling. The fire from their initial kiss tonight was back, ignited with a passion he didn't know was possible.

When he broke the kiss, he cupped each side of her face and waited until she locked eyes with him. "I love you, Willa. And when I get back, we will be figuring this out. I won't lose you. If I have to friendzone myself, permanently, I will. But you are it for me, Willa Claire Evans. This was—is—just the starting point." He kissed her again before he stood, holding his hand out for her. "Come to bed. I want to just be with you. Please?"

She grabbed his hand and followed him into the bedroom.

THREE HOURS LATER, Willa found herself standing on the airfield, wrapped in Declan's arms.

They already had his bags loaded and were given one last chance to say goodbye to loved ones.

"I'll be back in six months, okay?"

She studied his features—the sharp lines of his face, the bright blue eyes that captured her heart. Running a hand through his soft hair, she said, "Okay."

Why did this deployment feel so different from his last one? A part of her, deep down, felt like she was saying goodbye to him. To this version of him. She hated that feeling. She was in the Air Force herself, for God's sake. She could handle a deployment.

"Can you do me a favor?" He asked.

"Of course. Anything."

"That ivory dress you wore last night? Wear it to my homecoming, won't you?"

She smiled weakly. She could feel the buildup of sadness coming. "If you insist."

"Lean on Sofia and Cruz, okay?" He pressed his lips urgently to hers. "I love you, Evans."

Willa grabbed a fistful of his hair, pulling his lips to hers again. She truly couldn't get enough of his taste. She wanted to taste it forever. "I love you too, Hawke." Another quick kiss. "Now go kick some ass."

Chapter Eight

Six Weeks Later

DECLAN LOOKED AT Parker—his brother in every way except biological parents. Parker looked exactly like him all the way down to the identical birthmark on their shoulder. Even at twenty-six, the similarities between them would forever be eerie.

Parker knew about how Declan and Willa became friends, but when he showed up in Declan's living quarters, dropping his bag on the bed beside his, he knew something had happened between him and Willa, and had been harping on him for the last six weeks. An intuition was his exact words.

He was grateful that they lucked out and were put together on this deployment and were teamed up. They worked best when they were together; they always had been, but times like this, he wished that weren't the case. Even if all he needed was not to be hounded about the life that awaited him when he returned home.

"C'mon, man. You can't keep these details to yourself."

"I don't ask you about your sex life with Maddie." Declan shot back. He dragged his attention back to his laptop, refreshing his browser, hoping for an email from Willa. They were communicating regularly; the internet connection was luckily decent here, although they both avoided the topic of what was brewing between them, wanting to stick to their word and discuss it once he was home.

"If you asked, you'd know. I please my woman." Parker tapped a finger to his chin before snapping his fingers together. "Is *that* it? You don't want to talk about it because you're shit in bed?"

Declan grabbed his charger from his bed and threw it at his cousin. "Shut the fuck up. There is absolutely nothing wrong with my skills."

FaceTime popped up on Parker's laptop—an incoming call from Maddie. "We're going to continue this conversation in a minute." He accepted the call. "Hey, babe. I was just about to call you."

"No, he wasn't," Declan called from his bed; Parker shot him the middle finger.

"Hi Declan," Maddie said, laughing.

"Hey, Mads. Give Porter a kiss for me." He said, mentioning their one-year-old son. He turned his attention back to his laptop when his browser reflected an unopened email from Willa.

Smiling to himself, he opened it.

Dec,

I hope all is well. We're 45 days deep. Honestly wish it was 45 days left. So much shit has happened since you left. I ran into your pal Maddox at the commissary this morning. He's freaking out because he got someone pregnant. I'm sure that doesn't surprise you.

. . .

"Holy shit, are you serious?"

Declan looked up at Parker. His face was lit up with pride. "Everything okay?"

Parker beamed at Declan; his eyes were glassy with tears. "I'm going to be a daddy again!"

Holy shit. "Congratulations!"

A dad of two? Parker's attention already turned back to his computer, wiping at his eyes. A quick smile spread across his own face. If anyone deserved a big, happy family, it was Parker and Maddie.

A knock came at the entrance to the room. Declan turned his attention to the man standing in the doorway. "What's up, Paine?"

"Draper needs us. We're rolling out."

Fuck. Looks like their morning off just got fucked. Declan closed his laptop, reminding himself to reply to it when they got back.

"Babe, I gotta go," Parker said.

"Okay. You're the best part of me. I love you." Maddie answered.

"I love you three. You are my everything." He pressed his lips to the computer before shutting it.

They quickly changed before they headed out.

"YOU STILL HAVEN'T spilled on what is going on with you and Willa," Parker complained.

"Got yourself a girl back home, Hawke?" Bennett said from behind Parker in the Humvee.

Dec turned his eyes away from what he was doing to shoot him a glare. Not that he saw, all four men wore sunglasses to shield their eyes.

"Lay off him," Morris said from behind him.

"Thank you." God, why did Parker have to bring this up now? He needed to get to their destination and would much rather talk about Willa later.

"No problem." Morris clapped him on the shoulder. "Just let us know what we need to buy for your bachelorette party."

They busted up laughing.

"But seriously. Is this the girl you're always talking about?" Morris asked. "What's her name? Wilma—"

"Willow, right?" Bennett asked.

"Her name is Willa," Parker added. "And our boy Hawke here is in love."

Damn right he was, and he couldn't wait for this deployment to be over to tell her.

"How about we talk about how Rowe here knocked up his wife again." Please, anything for a change of subject.

Declan focused on the familiar rumble of the engine, now that the conversation turned.

"No shit! That's awesome, congrats, man." Bennett said.

"When did you find out?" Morris asked.

"Just before—"

The explosion came without warning, a blinding flash followed by an earth-shattering roar. The force of the blast lifted the Humvee off the ground, hurling it through the air like a toy. Declan's world spun violently, the cacophony of metal tearing and glass shattering drowning out all other sounds. Time seemed to slow as he felt himself thrown against the interior, the steering wheel slipping from his grasp.

The Humvee hit the ground with a bone-jarring impact, skidding and rolling before finally coming to a halt, a twisted wreck of smoking metal. Declan's vision swam as he tried to make sense of the chaos around him. Pain shot through his body, every breath a struggle. He could hear strained groans around him, a reminder that they were all still alive, if only barely.

Coughing through the thick smoke, Declan forced his eyes open. The interior of the Humvee was a nightmare of shattered glass and crumpled metal. The acrid smell of burning fuel stung his nostrils, and he could feel the searing heat from the flames licking at the edges of the vehicle.

They needed to get out. Now.

"Everyone okay?" He called out, his ears ringing. He wasn't even sure he'd be able to hear anyone.

"Bennett's out." *Fuck.*

Declan turned to check Parker. "Park!" Declan rasped, reaching out with a trembling hand to check on Parker. His cousin was slumped over, blood trickling down his face.

Fuck. Fuck. Fuck.

"We…need to…get out," he managed to gasp, his voice weak.

With a surge of desperate energy, Declan clawed at the door, his right arm shot bouts of pain throughout his body—he knew that pain; had felt it once before when he was nine. He forced the door open with a final grunt.

He staggered out, struggled to pull Parker out with him, stopping only when he got both of them a few feet away from the wreckage.

Parker lay on the ground, unmoving. *Fuck. Parker.*

He looked to his left, saw Morris had done the same with Bennett, who lay lifeless on the sand. The rest of the convoy had stopped, soldiers pouring out of their vehicles, weapons drawn, scanning for the source of the attack.

Declan's vision blurred again, his head swimming as he fought to stay conscious. He could hear voices shouting, orders being barked, but it all seemed distant, almost like he was underwater. He clung to the sand, the feel of it grounding him amid the chaos.

"Parker."

He had to be safe. He had to be alive.

As the medics reached them, Declan's grip on reality began to slip; the pain and shock finally overwhelmed him. The last thing he saw before darkness claimed him was the burning husk of the Humvee, and Parker's lifeless body—a stark reminder of how quickly everything could change.

DANCING ALONG TO Harry Styles, Willa stirred the chicken and noodles on the stove. She had been craving a family comfort meal, and Isabella's, although not her grandmother by birth, chicken and noodles with homemade mashed potatoes were just what she needed.

She put the wooden spoon down for the noodles, to check her phone for a text from Sofia. They planned on having a girls' day, watching romcoms, and drinking some wine. The last time they spent a day together was when Declan left for his deployment. Sighing, she looked at the calendar she had on her wall—fifty-three days down, a hundred and forty-two to go. She let out a sigh.

She couldn't wait. She let herself wallow for a few days after he left, just needing to get all of the emotions out and come to terms with what happened that night. It took her a solid week to be fully on board.

Her main focus was to keep counting down the days until he was in her arms, and they could be together.

She loved Declan and was completely ready to take that step from friendship to relationship. They could start their forever. She only hoped he came home feeling the same.

When she heard her door being unlocked, she turned, expecting Sofia's big announcement of her arrival, but she didn't find Sofia.

It was Declan.

"Dec?"

Her heart raced as she noticed his right arm in a sling. She turned her attention to his face, taking in the small cuts and the bruise that discolored his cheekbone.

His eyes, once vibrant, now appeared hollow and dull. The haunted expression etched upon his features tugged at her heart, filling her with a deep ache.

"Oh my God, Declan." He dropped his bags as she ran to him, wrapping her arms around him with caution, mindful of his injured arm. "What happened?"

He said nothing, just wrapped his good arm around her, pulling her into him so tight she was momentarily surprised she could still breathe. She felt his knees buckle beneath him, and she sank to the floor with him as he buried his face in her shoulder. He shuddered, and she could sense the tears beginning to fall.

She didn't say anything, didn't push him. She racked her memory through all the news articles she had read since he left, hoping she'd never see his name appear. It never did, so she thought he'd be fine. Whatever had happened to him overseas, he wasn't named, and she was thankful that he made it home alive.

NUMBNESS. THAT'S ALL he felt.

It had been eight days of hell.

Eight days ago, he and Parker were attached at the hip once again, giving each other shit over pointless things.

Eight days ago, Parker learned he was going to have a second baby.

Maddie was now a widow.

Porter was fatherless.

That baby will never even meet their father.

He gripped Willa as tight as he could, afraid that if he let go, she'd disappear too.

DECLAN HADN'T LEFT Willa's apartment for four days. He barely talked, barely ate. She knew he was just going through the motions at this point.

She wondered what had happened. She hadn't asked, hadn't wanted to push him to find out why he was back so soon. She recognized the profound shifts within him. The few times she managed a smile out of him, it never quite reached his eyes, and the shadows that danced beneath them told her that he was barely sleeping—not that she could blame him.

She sat on the couch with him now, his head in her lap. From the sounds of his rhythmic breathing, she knew he was asleep. It was rare at this moment, and she'd happily stay on the couch knowing he was at peace, even for a little while.

As she ran her fingers through his hair, she was

full of gratitude that he was home. That he was safe. The knowledge brought her solace, a balm to the gnawing anxiety that had started to consume her since he left. Even though he hardly spoke, she found comfort in knowing that he was here; that certainty was a lighthouse in the storm of her emotions.

WILLA JUMPED UP at the sound of metal hitting the floor, jolting her out of sleep.

She rubbed at her eyes, not realizing she had dozed. Her mind cleared when she realized Declan wasn't on the couch.

She looked around the apartment to find him walking into the kitchen, the rest of his things in his hands.

"Declan?"

He shoved his things in his bag carelessly before he turned, looking for something.

Willa pushed off the couch and walked to him. "Declan." He jumped when she placed a hand on his shoulder. "Are you okay?

"I need to go."

What?

"What do you mean? Where are you going?" She couldn't let him leave. Not like this.

"Home."

"Oh, okay. Let me drive you." She turned to grab her car keys and slip on her sandals.

"No. Like…" he dragged a hand through his hair as

he looked at her. His eyes were wild with earnestness. "Utah. I need to go to Utah."

"Oh."

"I'm sorry. I can't be here anymore. I need to go be with my family."

"Are you sure?"

She didn't understand why the sudden urgency.

He nodded, slipping on his shoes. "I am. I'm sorry. But I need to go home. I need to be with Maddie. She's all alone now. Just her and Porter."

Who in the world was Maddie? Who was Porter?

"Dec—"

"Oh God, the baby too." He looked at her again, but she knew he didn't see her. "What if she loses the baby in her grief?"

Willa didn't understand who he was talking about, but knew that, in time, he'd fill her in.

"I'll drive you to the airport, okay?" It's the least she could do.

"I bought tickets a few minutes ago. Payne knows as well. I'm not going AWOL."

"O-okay. Good, I'm glad you sorted it out."

"You'll drive me?" He asked, throwing his backpack over his shoulder.

"Of course I will."

He closed the distance between them and kissed her forehead. She closed her eyes and savored the moment. "Thank you, Willa. I need to take care of Maddie and the kids right now. It's what Parker would've wanted."

Parker. She needed to remember that name. He must've been involved in the accident that injured Declan, and most likely lost his life in the process. She wanted to look into it, but was afraid of what she might find.

She grabbed his other bag and hefted it over her shoulder.

Declan grabbed her arm, stopping her. "I can't thank you enough for these last few days. I needed it more than I can explain."

"It's never a problem, Dec. You're always there when I need you the most. I'm always here for you."

"I promise I'll explain what happened, okay? I just…" he trailed off, cleared his throat. "I just can't do that right now."

She nodded. "I understand, Declan. Come on. Let's get you home to your family."

Chapter Nine

Present Day

WILLA COULDN'T STOP her leg from bouncing.

After a six-month deployment, she was mere minutes away from Sofia's house to *finally* meet their newest baby girl, Hannah.

She smiled to herself, thinking about how her party girl best friend was now a happily married woman and a mom of *three* little girls. How quickly things changed.

After she stopped at their house, she had full intentions of stopping by Declan's apartment. She missed him like crazy and couldn't wait to be wrapped in his arms.

It took him a solid two years of fighting his demons alone before he was finally ready to tell her about what happened during his previous deployment.

She knew that he'd need to see her just as much as she needed him, even if all he needed was to touch her to know she made it back safely. She hoped that her surprise of coming home early was good and wouldn't send him into overdrive.

The Lyft driver stopped in front of the gorgeous brick home. She thanked the man after grabbing her bags and headed up the sidewalk to Sofia's house.

She knew Sofia had left the door unlocked for her,

just in case she was putting the baby down for a nap when she arrived. Dropping her bags in the front room, she headed towards the back of the house, where she found her friend.

Sofia was facing away from her, knuckles deep in kneading bread dough. *The perfect little housewife.* Willa loved seeing how much her friend had changed. She never wanted to be the type to settle down so young, but the life suited her, and Sofia wore it with pride.

A pang of envy fluttered in her stomach.

What I'd give to finally have that.

She and Declan never had the conversation about what happened and where they wanted their relationship to go. First the deployment, then the accident. Declan was still in therapy even after four years, and although it hurt her to do so, she left the possibility of a relationship on the back burner because she wanted him to focus on his mental health.

When Sofia dropped her bread dough into its pan to rise, Willa knocked on the wall. "Guess who?"

Sofia turned, wiping her hands on a towel, avoiding getting any on the fast-asleep, newest raven-haired baby on her chest that she wore on her chest. "Oh. My. God! Get your ass over here!"

Willa beamed and met Sofia halfway, pulling her into a hug, being careful not to squish the baby. "I missed you so much. Oh, look at her!" She looked at the baby and pressed a quick kiss to her head. "She looks just like her sisters did as an infant. I can't believe you have another baby."

She was so overwhelmed with emotions; she felt the tears pricking at her eyes.

"Oh no, are you okay?" Sofia asked, pulling her in for another hug, Hannah shifting between them.

Willa wiped at her eyes. "I'm fine. Honestly. I'm just so glad to be home. I've missed you all."

"Let me go put her down and give you a proper hug. I feel like we both need it."

"I'M GOING TO stop at the park before we head back to the house. The girls need to run off some steam. Hopefully, we can get them down for a nap." Cruz said.

"Sounds good," Declan agreed. "Hopefully Del can run off some steam, too. I'm sure he needs a nap too."

"Excuse me, old man," his brother complained from the backseat. "You're the one who probably needs a nap."

Declan shook his head. He was really glad that Delaney was able to make it to town so last minute. Willa was due home next week, and he was so anxious that he needed something to take his mind off her return.

He was determined to tell her how he felt. After his last deployment, they never talked about what had happened before he left, and the longer they went without talking about it, the bigger the hole in his heart felt.

He was going to propose to her. As soon as they had a minute alone. He didn't want to waste any more time. It was now or never.

He was ready to start his life with her—he only hoped she felt the same way.

He just hoped she made it home safely. He didn't know if he could handle losing her like he did Parker.

Once they were stopped at the park, everyone filed out, letting the girls run free since no one else was there.

"Uncle Dec! Play!" Holly shrieked.

He turned his attention to his three-year-old goddaughter. Her curly black hair bounced as she jumped.

"Oh, okay. I'll give you a five-second head start!" He jumped towards them. "You better run, squirts!"

Both girls screamed as they turned to run towards the giant play castle. Declan smiled as he watched them.

Even after all these years, he couldn't believe how much you could love someone else's child. He talked to Porter and Millie a few times a week—partially out of guilt for them losing their dad, but because he genuinely loved them and loved talking to them. Cruz and Sofia's girls were no different.

Hell, he volunteered to watch them when Sofia went into labor with Hannah and was the first non-family member to hold her. As soon as he could, he snapped a selfie holding her and emailed it to Willa to rub it in her face. Even now, it gave him a good laugh.

Having given the girls more than enough time, he

jogged towards them, ready to find them. Haley released a high-pitched shriek when he found her hiding in the slide. He hoisted her onto his shoulders as they ran around the wooden structure in search of Holly.

Haley screamed when she caught a glimpse of her sister running towards the screams. He took off after her, unable to help the laughter that bubbled out of him, as he closed the space between Holly and himself, releasing a hand from Haley to scoop the older girl in his arms as she laughed and called for her dad.

HE LOST TRACK of how long they played. They swung. They slid. He was exhausted.

He looked over at Cruz to see if he was ready to wrap it up. He and Del were deep into conversation, as Cruz checked his phone.

"Hold on a sec, okay?" He said to Holly as he jogged over to them.

"She is going to surprise the hell out of him," Cruz said, not seeing Declan approaching.

"She wasn't supposed to be back for another week, right?"

"Yeah. That's why we stopped. Willa wanted to be at the house to surprise Dec."

Willa. She was home. *Why the fuck was he at a* park?

"We're leaving. Now." He said, catching Cruz and Delaney in surprise. "Holly! Haley! Let's go home!"

The girls screamed in excitement and raced towards them.

"Were you not going to tell me about Willa being home?" His heart raced in his chest.

Willa, *his* Willa, was home.

She was safe.

She didn't die.

He wasn't going to be alone, and he wouldn't let his demons win. Not this time.

He needed to see her now.

Declan scooped up both girls and jogged them back to the car, anxious to get to the Pendolas' home.

HE RUSHED CRUZ home, Delaney chuckling in the back seat the whole ride.

Declan's phone had buzzed the entire way back, no doubt from the sibling group chat. He didn't need their shit right now.

What he needed was to get the fuck to Cruz's house and see Willa.

When Cruz pulled into the driveway, Declan was already unbuckled and had his door open before the SUV came to a complete stop. He heard both men laughing as he forced the door open.

He ran through the foyer, past the front room where Willa's bags were dropped off.

When he entered the kitchen, his breath caught in his throat. There stood Willa, clad in a soft blue tank top and denim shorts, her bare feet on the cool blue tiles. Her hair was swept back into a clip. Beside her, Sofia stood, guiding Willa as she scored a loaf of bread.

Both oblivious to his presence, he stood—unmoving—as his heart pounded in his chest.

Willa was here. In the flesh.

He felt tears prick in his eyes.

"Mama!" Haley and Holly shouted as they ran inside.

Sofia turned to her girls first, catching Declan's eye as she bent down to kiss her daughters.

Willa followed suit but stopped when she saw him.

Her face lit up with an infectious smile.

She was home. She was alive.

In that instant, everything else faded into oblivion. There was only Willa.

His feet seemed to move of their own accord as he walked toward her, a wave of emotion overtook him—an overwhelming urge to embrace her, to feel her warmth and anchor himself in the reality of her presence.

Had he been that worried that she wouldn't make it home? Sure, he had been worried, but he hadn't realized how much it weighed on him.

As he wrapped his arms around her waist, the anxiety and tension melted away. He buried his face in her shoulder, inhaling the familiar scent of her—lilac and lemons—a scent that had become home for him.

Tears filled his eyes as he squeezed her tight. "I missed you so much." He whispered, his voice shaky. "You have no idea how much."

Declan pulled back slightly, his hands lingering on her waist as he searched her face. She looked good. She looked *perfect*.

"I'm so glad you're back." He couldn't stop himself. He needed the constant reassurance that she was fine.

"I'm happy to be back," she replied, her voice thick with emotion.

He wiped a tear from the corner of her eye before he kissed her forehead and pulled her in for another hug.

SEEING THE RELIEF on Declan's face when she locked eyes with him had her heart aching.

She understood why.

Deployments are already hard enough—whether someone is being shipped out or left behind—but being on the other side of a traumatic accident like he was involved in. She understood the anxiety he had to overcome in the last six months.

When they broke apart, she bent down to give Holly and Haley their hugs and followed the welcome by getting a hug from Cruz.

She loved her unconventional family and was thankful that she was able to have a welcome home like this.

What she didn't expect was the man who stood in the doorway watching the reunion.

He was the same height and build as Declan. His

hair tousled; his bright blue eyes sparkled as he took in his surroundings.

He locked eyes with her, his mouth turned lopsided as he gave her a half smile.

"Hey," she said. Unsure what Hawke brother he was, she took a chance. "Delaney, right?"

"First try, very nice." He walked to her, pulled her in for a hug, as Sofia shuffled the girls out of the room for a nap. "I have been waiting seven long years to meet you, Willa. Welcome home."

"Th—thank you." She stammered. "In town for a visit?"

"I am. Declan here," he clapped his brother on the shoulder. "Was lonely. Apparently, his hand wasn't giving him enough company anymore. So he asked me to come out for a few days until you returned."

"Man, shut the fuck up." Declan scolded him.

Willa couldn't help the laugh that escaped. "I'm glad you could keep him company. And that he's giving his hand a rest."

Delaney hollered with laughter. "I like you. Dec, you need to wife her up already or I'm going to beat you to it."

She beamed at him as Declan glared at his little brother.

Chapter *Ten*

THEY WENT TO Club Thirst to celebrate Willa's return.

What else were they going to do?

Sofia and Cruz had already lined up a babysitter, wanting to be carefree for the night. The joke of them making baby number four happened more than once.

Willa lost track of how much she drank. She wasn't the biggest drinker, but for this? She was happy to oblige.

After all, she was celebrating her safe return, the birth of Hannah, and what she failed to mention to anyone else, she was also drinking to work up the courage to *finally* tell Declan how she felt about him.

They were seven years overdue.

She laughed at all of Delaney's fifth-wheel jokes, while Declan groaned at them. He tried, more than once, to get Del to go find some poor woman to hook up with so he'd leave them the fuck alone.

Del was her newest buddy, and she was not standing for it, which, she knew, probably infuriated Declan—at least a little.

He kept a hand on her all night; the only time that contact broke was when one of them needed to use the restroom, and they couldn't physically be together.

Although she wanted nothing more than to drag him into one of the rooms and fuck him thoroughly.

It had been so long since she had sex, she was willing to climb him and ride him on the dance floor.

Thankfully, she wasn't *that* drunk.

When Sofia and Cruz headed home at midnight, Declan, Delaney, and Willa decided to head back to Declan's apartment since he lived only a few blocks away.

They had a few drinks at the apartment, Declan wanting to do a few toasts in honor of Willa's safe return. The emotion in his voice confirmed that he had been worried during her absence.

AT SOME POINT, Willa found herself on Declan's couch, her body warm and relaxed from the alcohol.

She needed tonight. Needed to let loose and be carefree for a while.

Her head rested on Declan's lap, while Delaney lay sprawled out on the floor, like a starfish stuck to a rock.

She was soaking up the silence, half asleep when Del said, "You two should elope."

Her eyes shot open, and she snapped her neck towards him. "What?"

"Why?" Declan asked.

He lifted his head off the floor to look at them. "Yeah. I mean, why not?"

Why not?

Why *shouldn't* they get married? She was in love

with him and wanted to be with him. He said he loved her too. It may not be in the same way, but he could grow to feel that way, too, right?

She looked from Del to Declan, his eyes on his brother, shock evident on his face.

Maybe he didn't feel the same way.

After a moment, he blinked and looked at her. The expression in his eyes told her he wanted this as much as she did.

Either she had too much to drink, or his eyes told her that he wanted it too.

"I don't hate the idea." He said to her.

Delaney added, "You two are grossly in love anyway. Instead of doing something about it and getting regular sex, you're both just…" he trailed off, waving a hand at them as he dropped his head back onto the floor.

Willa stared at Declan, willed him to feel the same way.

"Happy fuckin' like rabbits ever after," Del mumbled.

"Let's do it," Declan said to her.

She shot up, her head spinning at the sudden movements, as she turned towards him. "For real?"

"In Del's famous words, yeah, why not?" He smiled.

Shit. Yes. Please.

"Yes! Let's go!" She jumped to her feet, sobering up enough to know she'd remember.

It made her feel a little guilty, but this was what she had wanted for years, and suddenly, it was within reach. She'd just have to fake it.

"Fuck. Yes." Del said, rolling over to get up. Willa

closed the distance to him, helped him stand before she pressed a quick kiss to his cheek in thanks.

DECLAN STOOD AT the altar in Love on the Run, the only twenty-four-hour business in the area.

How ironic was that?

He sobered up when they agreed to do this. The biggest life alteration, and he was going to be sober for it, even if he did have to fake it a little.

Delaney took it upon himself to be the witness, photographer, best man, and even told Willa he'd fuck Dec up as her maid of honor.

He smiled as he watched his little brother, as drunk as he was, snapping away; taking pictures of the room, Declan, and even himself.

He *may* have been a little annoyed at Del for ruining his plan, but it got him to the finish line faster, so why would he complain? He owed his brother everything.

He thanked Delaney more times than he could count for pushing them to do this. Something Declan had been teetering on for years. Now, they were going to finish what they started three years ago, and he couldn't fucking wait.

Declan shifted on his feet, anticipation waiting for

Willa. She told him that despite their eloping, she wanted to give a grand entrance.

He ran his hands down his shirt, the smooth blue dress shirt she made him put on because she was *not* going to marry him while he wore a t-shirt for his favorite movie.

Even she made their Lyft driver take them to her apartment on the way to Love on the Run so she could grab a dress.

Drunk and eloping, she was going to do it right in her own eyes.

The officiant's wife came out to start the wedding march, and his palms went sweaty immediately.

He pulled the sapphire engagement ring out of his pocket. The one he bought on a whim a few years ago, with the plan to give it to her when he finally got the balls to make a move.

Simple silver wedding bands were included in their elopement package, but he wanted to surprise her by giving her the engagement ring too.

The music started, and his breath caught in his throat.

Willa walked around the corner, holding a small bouquet of soft pink roses, wearing *the* ivory dress that had been in his dreams for three years.

The way she smiled at him told him she knew exactly how he felt about the dress, and that was her reason for picking it tonight.

Declan didn't recall a single word the officiant said.

He saw only Willa.

He heard only Willa.

He said his lines when she squeezed his hand.

He saw the shock on her face when he slid not only the wedding band on her finger, but followed it with the stunning sapphire ring.

Tears streamed down his face as she slid the wedding band onto his finger, its simple metal encasing the weight of his entire world.

As the officiant pronounced them husband and wife, Declan felt an electric rush shoot through him.

He cupped her cheek with one hand, bunched his hand at her back just above the swell of her ass, and pulled her to him, surrendering to the gravity of the moment.

Their lips met in a kiss that was soft and powerful, tender yet full of intensity. He felt a rush of warmth flood over him as if every dream and hope he had for this future with her was poured into this moment.

As they pulled away, he dropped his forehead to hers, as Delaney, the officiant, and his wife erupted into applause. He was thankful for Delaney coming to visit, for giving them this idea, and he was grateful that he was sober enough to remember this.

They turned together, beaming with love, as Delaney snapped picture after picture, making sure to get close-ups of their rings and every detail he felt was important enough to remember.

THEY LEFT LOVE on the Run shortly after, everyone high on the rush of what they just did.

"I can't believe we just did that! We're MARRIED!"

Willa said, swinging her arms around Declan's neck, kissing him.

He felt himself melt into her before she pulled away when their phone's texting alert went off simultaneously.

Who would be texting them in the middle of the night?

Declan held onto Willa as he pulled out his phone, new messages from the group chat, *Sibling Shenanigans +1.*

DEL

Look what just happened! I'm clearly the favorite since I was the only one allowed to come.

DEMPSEY

Why are you waking me up?

That's when the pictures popped up on Declan's phone.

Oh no. Declan looked at Willa before he scrolled through them.

Del said he'd send them to just the two of them. But there they all were.

DEMPSEY

What. The. Fuck?!

TALIA

Oh my god! WHAT

TAELYN

Declan?! Willa!? EXPLAIN

"Del..." Declan started.

His brother turned around; his eyes still glossy.

"What?"

"You just told our sisters and brother."

Declan watched his brother's face sober up as he looked at his phone again.

"Whoops."

Chapter *Eleven*

"SO, I MAY have fucked up more than we originally thought."

Willa opened her eyes, blinking against the harsh light, taking a long moment to realize she *wasn't* overseas, but she was in Declan's room.

The light green of his walls told her as much.

Wait.

She shot up, staring at her hand, taking in the ring that was *most definitely* there. The one-and-a-half-carat oval sapphire ring was the focal point of the stunning ring. Its deep blue color mesmerizing and captivating, drawing the eye in and holding it there. Two delicate diamonds on each side of the sapphire added an extra touch of sparkle to the look. The rose gold band, with its pink hues, added a romantic touch to the design, intertwining in an infinity shape. Two additional, smaller sapphires on the band added an extra pop of color to the ring. Beside it sat a thin silver band.

Her breath quickened as last night came flooding back. Drinking with her friends, celebrating her return, followed by Delaney's idea for them to elope.

Holy shit. She really married the man she loved.

They really did elope last night—this morning?

She remembered leaving Club Thirst at midnight

when Sofia and Cruz did. It was definitely this morning.

"I doubt it was any worse than what you did last night," Declan grumbled as he rolled over onto his side towards her, wrapping his arm around her waist.

"Uhm," Delaney trailed off. Willa looked at him, arching an eyebrow. "I may have texted Mom and Dad, too."

Willa's eyes widened as she sat up, Declan doing the same.

"You…WHAT!" Declan shouted.

She covered her mouth to stifle the shock and the laughter that threatened to come out.

Why did she find that funny? She didn't know, but she couldn't help it.

"I *really* fucked up, didn't I?" Willa couldn't hold in the laughter anymore.

"What is so funny?" They both asked, which only threw her into another fit of laughter.

"I'm sorry," she said in between bursts of laughter. "I can't help it."

She wiped at her eyes as Declan pushed her back down onto the pillow.

"What exactly did you tell them?"

Delaney tossed his phone on the bed, clearly afraid to get too close to his brother.

Declan grabbed the phone that had the texting chain open for Del and their parents.

He sent them one photo. Declan had his lips pressed to hers, the smile still evident on their face, as Declan held her left hand out, showing off the sapphire ring.

With the way they were dressed, it looked like they

had just gotten engaged, and Delaney sent that to Norah and Connor. The text below it read, "Look what these two crazy cats did tonight!"

"They know we're married?" Declan asked, his voice quiet.

"No," Del started. "They think you're engaged. I woke up this morning, and my phone was blowing up from mom and dad. They have apparently been hounding the others, but no one has said anything. Thankfully."

Fuck.

"But you really need to talk to them. Before mom flies them here."

"She'll do it too," Declan muttered. "Fuck. What are we going to do?"

"That sounds like a 'you' problem, big bro. I'm going to—"

"The fuck you are," Declan said, jumping out of bed to stop his brother. "It was *your* idea. And *you* are going to help us figure this out."

Declan's phone began to ring. Willa leaned across the bed, picking up the phone. It was Norah.

"It's your mom," *and my mother-in-law.* The reality of that had her feeling wistful at the idea of having a mom.

She heard Declan suck in a breath. "We can't avoid her. What should we say?"

Willa looked at him and saw the worry in his eyes. "Why don't we just go along with it?"

Declan cocked an eyebrow. "Like, let them believe we're engaged?"

"Would you rather tell your mom we got married?" She felt a flutter in her stomach at her words.

"Mom would not be happy about that. Especially since you're the first of us to take the plunge." The ringing stopped.

"Again, no thanks to you."

Del just shrugged.

The way he said it, Willa wondered if he regretted it. She really hoped he didn't.

When his phone started ringing again, Norah's picture popped up again.

"Declan," she looked at him, understanding the worry on his face. She held his phone out to him. "I don't want Norah freaking out if you don't answer."

He hesitated before he nodded, taking the phone from her as he sat back down.

With a deep breath, he slid his thumb across the screen and answered.

OH, HE WAS fucking *nervous.*

The last time he was this nervous, he was sixteen and got busted sneaking out of the house.

He took a deep breath before he slid his thumb across the screen to accept his mom's FaceTime.

"Hey, Mom—"

"Declan Matthew Hawke," *Fuck.* "Why the hell did I

wake up this morning to a text message from Delaney saying you and Willa are *engaged?* I didn't even know you two were dating!"

Shit, what was he supposed to say?

Willa squeezed his thigh in support. He knew that whatever he said, she'd go along with.

So why not stick as close to the truth as possible?

"Sorry, Mom. We weren't exactly dating."

"Then how—"

"Let him talk, Norah." Connor appeared on screen, sitting on the couch next to his wife. His face brightened, the skin crinkling around his eyes as he smiled at Declan. "Hey, Son. I hear congratulations are in order."

"At least someone knows how to do a proper congrats," Delaney said from the door. Declan shot him a look before he flipped the phone around. Might as well give him his five minutes of fame. Delaney glared at Declan before he smiled. "Hey, Mom. Hey, Pops."

"Delaney, we will be talking after I'm done talking to your brother," Norah warned. Declan turned the phone back around, as Del stuck his tongue out before he disappeared.

Willa laughed silently beside him.

"So, what happened? Why did I get the text in the middle of the night? Where's Willa? I need to know everything!"

Connor began his attempt at mellowing Norah as Declan shifted on the bed, turning the phone sideways to bring Willa into view.

He felt her trembling slightly and wrapped his arm around her for the comfort he knew she needed.

"Ahh! Willa!" Norah yelled! "It's so good to see you! How was your deployment?"

"It was good. Uneventful, thankfully."

Declan squeezed her for his own comfort this time. He still couldn't believe she was back.

"So, tell me about the engagement. How did you go from friends to getting married?"

Actually married, he thought.

The truth. Stick to it as much as possible.

"Well, I decided shortly after she left that when she got home, I was going to pop the question. I felt like, where I was emotionally, we could skip the dating. A little unconventional, but I just had a feeling."

And he did. He had just hoped she would feel the same. Now that they were actually married, he wondered how she really felt when it came to him. To their new relationship.

"Oh, that is just so sweet," Norah said, her eyes bright with happiness. "We knew the two of you were going to end up together."

"We're surprised it finally happened," Connor added. "Declan's not the quickest when it comes to decisions."

Hurt, he stuck out his bottom lip. "Hey, I just wanted to be sure, thank you."

"I'm sure." Connor laughed.

"So, the engagement. Where did it happen? When? *How?*"

This is where it got sticky.

"Well," Willa started. She looked at him, searching for an answer.

"I had this whole plan. Flowers, music, candles. She wasn't supposed to be home until next week."

"I surprised him." She said, beaming at him.

He returned the smile. "She did. I couldn't believe it. But it was the best kind of surprise."

Willa bumped his shoulder with hers. "Everything about last night was the best." She turned to look at him, the most beautiful smile on her face—one that, if he let himself believe it, was genuine for what they did.

He was lost in Willa's gaze when he heard his mom clapping. "Oh, that is just so sweet. You two need to come back and visit."

He turned to the phone. "What?"

"Well, yeah. You're the first of my children to *finally* get married. You bring her home. Willa, you're on R and R, right?"

"Uh, yeah. I have two weeks starting tomorrow."

Oh no. He knew what his mom was getting at.

"Mom—"

"Declan, you get ahold of Payne, or I'll do it for you. We'll take care of the plane tickets."

Shit. She knew what strings to pull with Payne if he didn't do it too.

"I'll text him as soon as we're off the phone."

"Perfect. We'll clear our schedules and will see you in two days." She beamed. "I need to spend time with my future daughter-in-law and my son. Who doesn't come home often as he claimed he would." The gleam in her eyes had him shuddering.

He knew the last bit was a guilt trip, and it was a twist of the knife in his heart. It wasn't that he didn't want to see his family; he just would rather be here with Willa.

"Yeah. Okay. We'll see you in two days." *Fuck. Fuck. Fuck.*

"Love you both." Norah's smile was smug, pleased with herself for winning this battle.

"Love you." He said as he hung up, throwing his phone down on the bed. He turned to look at Willa.

He couldn't read her emotions. Was she happy? Anxious? Worried?

"I'm your wife. Pretending to be your fiancée." She said like she couldn't believe what had happened.

He dragged a hand through his hair, a little frustrated with himself. With Del. "I'm sorry."

"Why?"

"Because my idiot brother put us in this position to begin with, and now we have to go along with this."

She shrugged; her face still unreadable, the look had him feeling guilty for everything.

"We'll fix this, I promise." He saw a quick look of disappointment cross her face before she schooled her expression, and he wondered what it was about.

He didn't want to; he hoped that going to Utah would give him the time to prove to her how perfect they were for one another.

"Don't worry about it. We'll figure it out."

His mood perked. "You're okay with pretending to be my fiancée in front of my family? Where everyone but my parents know that we're actually married?"

"Of course. I think it'll be easier to fake a step backward than it would be had you drunkenly told them we were engaged." She smiled at him, humor dancing in her eyes.

That smile sent his heart fluttering.

"We need to talk to your siblings and tell them what's going on."

"We will," He said, nodding. "We'll make calls today. Deal?"

"Sounds good to me. But I just want to say, I will not be responsible if your parents find out."

"They'll never know." To seal the deal, he leaned in and pressed his lips to hers. She opened for him just enough to give him hope. "Welcome to the family, Willa Hawke."

He intended his words to be playful, but he didn't miss the small intake of breath when he muttered her new name.

Maybe there was hope after all.

Chapter Twelve

TWO DAYS LATER Willa, Declan, and Delaney sat at the airport waiting for their flight.

Willa was astonished that Declan was able to get leave approved so quickly. She asked how he was able to do it and all he would say was that Payne was a cool guy and understanding.

She had a feeling that there was more to it, but she didn't care enough to ask. She was just happy enough to be here with him and happy to see his family again.

She had never been to Bedpa, let alone Utah. She was a Midwesterner, coming from a small town in Indiana, and had only traveled through the states leading to Florida, where her family spent every vacation. She glanced out the windows, trying to catch glimpses of the mountains as they walked. She couldn't wait to get a full view of where Declan called home.

The only time she branched out from that routine was when she went to Texas for basic training, and Mississippi for technical school, before she was sent to North Carolina for her duty station. She loved the opportunities to see new places, even if she rarely left her usual places. She made a mental note to book more trips.

She sighed, sitting back as Declan grabbed her hand,

lacing his fingers with hers. She smiled at their hands, thinking about how they got here and how they were going to proceed after this trip. She wanted nothing more than to be able to convince him that they should be together like this.

"Are you okay?" He asked, putting his iPad down to look at her.

"I am. Little nervous, but I'm excited to see your parents again. Will I finally meet the others?"

"Probably. Knowing Mom, she's planning on a party or something." He looked at his watch. "Mom's birthday is next week, so I'm sure everyone will be home to celebrate. We always make sure to be with them on their birthdays."

Willa felt a pang of guilt. She made sure to call her dad on his birthday, but never thought to go see him. "That's so sweet. I guess I never realized you did that."

"Fun little tradition, I guess." He shrugged, not realizing how big a deal it was. She didn't have to be a parent to understand how important it was to Norah and Connor.

"I'm sorry to interrupt," Willa turned her attention from Declan to an elderly woman and her husband. "Did the two of you just get married? You're both positively glowing."

Declan beat her to it. "We did, on Friday."

Willa looked at him and could see the happiness on his face. She wondered if it was legitimate or if he was just putting on a show for the couple.

The woman put her hand on her heart. "What a special day. We celebrated our fiftieth anniversary on the second."

Willa's eyes widened. "Fifty? Wow. Congratulations!"

"I bet it was a beautiful wedding, too. My grandparents have been married for fifty-five years, and I love seeing pictures of their wedding." Declan commented.

The man laughed. "We don't have any wedding photographs."

"Well, not from *that* wedding anyway." She looked at Willa and Declan, her brown eyes sparkling. "We eloped."

"We had a little too much to drink. But we had been friends for a long time, and we both realized we were in love. That night, we got married." Her husband said.

No way. Willa looked at Declan, unable to hide the smile on her face.

"That's what happened to us, too." Declan returned the smile.

The couple laughed. Willa felt like she was looking at herself in the future with Declan still by her side. If this couple could do it, why couldn't they?

"Hold on tight to one another. Life is a wild ride, but having your best friend with you every step of the way. That's the best life anyone could ask for."

"Hey lovers, miss me?" Delaney asked as he sat down next to Willa, before passing out their drinks and snacks. Willa opened her water, let the cold water fill her mouth.

Delaney looked over at the elderly couple they had been talking to, "Did they tell you we're in a throuple?"

She almost spit out her water.

"Delaney," Declan groaned.

"We were, too. But he died, unfortunately." The

swift reply from the man had Willa bursting with laughter.

"Oh, so he ghosted you?" He deadpanned.

The man and woman both laughed before the wife said, "Same sense of humor, I see. We have a son who is just like you. Life of the party, center of attention."

"Makes you want to pull your hair out?" Declan asked.

"Once upon a time he did."

The attendant at the desk started calling boarding groups, stopping the conversation.

"It was nice to meet you," Willa said when they stood to line up.

They stopped collecting their bags to look at her and smiled. "You as well, dear. Don't let each other go. Have a wonderful life together."

Willa felt tears prickling in her eyes when Declan wrapped an arm around her. "She's stuck with me now."

"MY SWEET BOY!" Norah Hawke called out as she ran down the steps from her front door, loose tendrils of her blonde hair flying in the wind. If Willa hadn't met her already, she'd think Norah Hawke was in her late thirties. Willa smiled at the woman as she headed straight for Declan, who stepped out from the back of the vehicle to wrap his arms around her tightly. She felt her heart soften at the mother and son in their embrace.

"What about me?" Delaney whined as Declan pulled away from her, kissing one cheek then the other.

She turned her sharp blue eyes on him. "I'm still mad at you."

"You look great!" Declan said, trying to take the heat off of his brother.

Norah did a little spin, showing off the tan flowy pants and peach-colored blouse. Willa couldn't help but smile at the woman who was radiating happiness. What she would give to look that happy at her age.

"I've lost ten pounds, and I feel *fantastic*. Talia started making me go to Pilates, and it has done wonders for me." She shut the trunk door before walking around the car to Willa, pulling her into a hug. When they separated, Norah, with a gleam in her blue eyes. "It's done wonders for Connor and my sex life, too."

Willa turned her attention to Declan, who was picking up the bags he had placed on the driveway. "Mom," he and Delaney groaned together, making Willa laugh.

She looked back at his mom, who sent her a wink. *Oh, this is going to be fun.*

Del tossed his bag in his truck, grabbed a white cowboy hat, and placed it on his head. "I gotta head out. Chief texted."

"The fire in Wyoming?" Norah asked.

"Yep."

Norah walked to Del and pulled him into a hug. "Be safe. I love you. Pain in the ass, but I love you."

Del flashed her a smile as he waved to Declan and Willa. "Love you guys. Tell dad for me." He said as he hopped in his truck.

Norah walked back to Willa and started to lead her towards the house.

"Don't worry about me, I'll take the bags up to my room," Declan muttered as the women turned towards the house. Willa let out a chuckle as she sent him a little finger wave as she was being led away from him.

Willa was in awe of the house. The Rocky Mountains provided the perfect backdrop for the Hawke home, with tall trees and blooming flowers dotting the property. The house itself was a beautiful blend of rustic and modern architecture, the white exterior of the home perfectly complementing the natural surroundings with its natural stone and wood accents. As she stepped onto the porch, she pictured herself sitting in one of the rocking chairs, surrounded by several potted plants.

Stepping inside, Willa was amazed by the large windows that flooded the home with natural light, illuminating the spacious and welcoming interior. The open floor plan seamlessly connected the living, dining, and kitchen areas, creating a perfect space for the large Hawke family. The décor was a mix of rustic and modern, with comfortable furniture and tasteful accents that added to the sense of warmth and familiarity.

Norah stopped only when they reached the kitchen, pulling out a stool for Willa to sit. "Sweet tea fan, right?"

Willa smiled as she sat. "Yes, please. If it isn't too much trouble."

Norah turned to grab a glass, allowing Willa to take in the kitchen. It was a chef's dream, equipped with top-of-the-line appliances. The cabinets were painted a rich, dark green, and the countertops were butcher block. The kitchen sink was positioned along a large wall of windows that overlooked the expansive backyard. Outside, a sprawling patio and a beautiful, expansive, lush green lawn created the idyllic setting for outdoor relaxation and dining.

Willa felt longing as she took in the yard, and the kitchen, and found herself picturing being here often, Declan in the backyard with their kids—the thought had her heart pounding a little. She had to remind herself again that this was only temporary.

She sighed, running her hand along the cool concrete countertop of the large island, a stark contrast to the warmth of the rest of the kitchen.

"Gorgeous, isn't it?" Norah asked, placing the glass of tea in front of Willa.

"It is. I would never tire of it." She looked at Norah now and smiled. "I hope you haven't."

Norah shook her head. "Absolutely not. I have been fortunate enough to not need to work. I get to stay home and enjoy this view."

Willa took a sip of her tea, the flavor exploding in her mouth. "Have you always stayed home?"

"I have. When we first married, we lived in a small RV, right here on this land. Connor built this house for us, expanding when we needed."

"There was no house here before?"

"Nope. Connor's father gave it to us as a wedding gift. He hoped that Connor would take over the Hawke ranch eventually."

Willa thought over Norah's words. "Connor is a lawyer, right?"

The older woman smiled. "He is. Dodger may not have gotten his wish, but he's damn proud of his son—and all of his grandchildren. Connor helps out with the ranch when he can." Norah looked out the kitchen window. "He's actually on his way home now from the ranch."

Willa followed Norah's line of sight when she saw the older man jogging towards the house. Her lips curved at the sound of Norah's sigh. How that must feel, to be together as long as they had been and still be in love.

Connor entered the kitchen, immediately going to his wife, dropping his lips to hers. When they separated, he turned towards Willa. It never failed to shock her how similar Connor was to Declan, to all the Hawke siblings. They all hit the genetics jackpot.

He walked around the island to her now and wrapped his arms around her in a hug. "Willa! It's so good to see you. Have a safe flight?"

"We did," she said when the hug broke. "It's good to see you."

"Likewise, my girl." He said, looking between the two women as he walked to the refrigerator. "Where's Declan and Delaney?"

"Del is off to go fight in Wyoming," Norah said, smiling weakly at her husband as he pulled her in for a hug. Willa's heart ached. She couldn't imagine being the parent of not one but two children who put their lives on the line.

"He'll be fine," Connor said, releasing Norah. "What about Declan?"

"I'm here," he said, walking into the room, stopping beside Willa. "I took our bags up to our room." Declan bumped his hip against hers, flutters exploding in her stomach.

Why *was* she getting flutters over a hip bump? He was her best friend, for crying out loud. They were fucking *married*.

Pull yourself together, Willa.

"You were gone for a while," Norah commented, arching an eyebrow at him. From the eye roll he sent her way, Willa knew scoldings were a frequent occurrence for him. Most likely for all five of the Hawke kids, if she had to put money on it.

"Bathroom break, if you must know." He walked around the island to his father and wrapped his arms around him, patting Connor on the back. "Good to see you, Dad."

"Been too long. Have you been doing okay?" Connor asked as they separated.

Willa knew it was because of his accident. He had more good moments than bad, but she knew the PTSD from it crept up unexpectedly.

"Doing good," Declan turned with Connor's arm around his shoulder. "Better now."

He sent her a pointed look. It took her a moment to figure out why; she looked down at her hand that held the stunning engagement ring. They took off their wedding bands when they landed, covering the last of their tracks on their elopement.

Norah must've noticed the glance because she raced around the island to grab Willa's hand, studying the ring on her finger.

"Oh, Declan. This is absolutely stunning. Well done." Norah gushed as she held Willa's hand out to Connor for him to get a better look.

Willa let out a breath and looked Declan in the eye. His smile widened before he winked at her, turning his attention back to his mom.

She felt bad for lying to Connor and Norah, but she hoped and prayed it would all work out in the end.

Chapter Thirteen

"I'M GOING TO hop in the shower before dinner, wash off the travel. Need anything?" Dec asked as they walked into his bedroom sometime later.

Willa shook her head. "I think I'm good. Is it okay if I unpack? I don't want to live out of my suitcase while we're here." In just the short amount of time they had been here, her emotions had been all over the place. For some reason, she was struggling to process how she ended up in Utah, married, but pretending that she was engaged.

Life—was absolutely wild.

She needed to put herself through a menial task, using it to ground herself.

"Definitely not. Make yourself comfortable. I took the left side of the dresser if you want the right. They're all empty." She looked at the wooden dresser and nodded.

"That's perfect, thank you."

He stepped to her, closing the distance between them. "You never have to thank me, Willa. What's mine is yours, *wife*." She sucked in a breath at the way he said it. We're family, after all."

She nodded. *Family. Wife. Right.*

He kissed her temple before he walked towards the

adjacent bathroom, closing the door behind him, before she heard the shower start.

With a heavy sigh, she made her way to the bed, grabbed her suitcase, and dropped it on the luscious gray comforter. She noted the bed frame matched the dresser, desk, and side tables that sat on either side of the bed. She took in the soft blue walls that rivaled Dec's captivating eye color. The walls were sparsely adorned with a few band posters and framed photographs. Willa smiled when she noticed the framed photo of the two of them together on his twenty-fourth birthday.

The memory of their FaceTime call when he added the picture to his wall. He told her she was a permanent part of his life and deserved a spot in his childhood room. She loved that he had done that. Proud to show off their friendship.

Unzipping her bag, she started pulling out her clothes, noting the racier lingerie that was packed. She smirked, thinking about her conversation with Sofia yesterday about how she needed to make the move into solidifying their relationship. Willa hoped she had the opportunity to tease him with it, even if it appeared innocent.

She unpacked slowly, trying to lose her mind in the task. When she reached her favorite zip-up hoodie—purple with a snake wrapped around the right arm that Sofia had given her fifteen years ago—she picked it up, when a purple vibrating dildo fell out of the hoodie.

She picked it up, still in its packaging, with a Post-It on it reading:

In case Dec isn't satisfying enough.
- Cruz & Sof

Willa felt her face redden. She knew that this was how they could be, but *damn it,* she hadn't expected this. When would Sofia have had the time to do this?

She thought back to yesterday when Sofia was at her apartment. The only time she hadn't been in the room with Sofia was when the pizza was delivered.

Immediately, she grabbed her phone and dialed Sofia.

"A fucking *vibrator?*" Willa hissed, hoping no one else would hear her.

Sofia's laugh filled the speaker. "You're welcome."

"Why would I need this? What were you thinking?" She picked up the packaging and forced herself not to laugh when she saw they had taped a photo of Declan's head to the top of it. She needed to be mad. She wanted to be mad.

The conversation with Dec about why she even had it flashed in her head. She knew if he found out, he'd never let her live it down.

"Holly had gotten ahold of my phone a few weeks ago and had ordered it without me realizing. We don't have an issue with our sex life—obviously, look at the three kids we have—but thought it would be good for you, and possibly Dec if we sent it to good ol' Utah with the two of you."

"Not like it's going to get used."

Sofia tsked. "Nonsense. Why not have a little fun while you're there?"

"Because," Willa stepped closer to the bathroom to check to see if the shower was still running. She did *not* need Declan walking in on this conversation. "We're not really together. You know this."

A poor excuse, but it's all she had.

Her friend was silent on the other line, and Willa checked to make sure she hadn't hung up. "No. What I do know is that two of my best friends, who are in love with one another, are just too afraid to act on it, despite them wanting the same thing. The fact that Declan's *brother* even sees this and managed to convince the two of you to elope should be more than enough proof of that. The vibrator was just something funny I couldn't resist doing. Besides," she paused. "I'm *positive* Declan doesn't need a vibrator. He has got to know what he's doing by now."

Willa noticed the bathroom door had opened slightly. *He must not have closed it properly.* She went to close the door when she peered inside as he turned the shower off. From the angle that they stood, she could see him, clearly, in the mirror, his cock half hard. "Holy shit." She muttered.

"What?" Sofia asked as Declan's eyes flew up, meeting her gaze in the mirror. She jumped back, slamming her hip into the edge of the bedside table, before she rushed back to her suitcase, grabbed the vibrator, and shoved it in the drawer with her shirts.

Fuck, fuck, fuck.

"He saw me." She whispered to Sofia.

"He saw you what?" Her friend demanded.

"I gotta go," Willa said, hanging up, Sofia's voice calling out for her. She shoved her phone back in her pocket as she practically ran to the door, hoping to avoid him. Maybe if she wasn't in the room when he walked out, he'd think that he was mistaken on seeing her. *One could only hope.*

She turned to close the door behind her as she entered the hallway. Before she could take more than two steps, she collided with a bare-chested man with a striking tattoo stretched across his chest. The tattoo depicted a dark and turbulent scene with swirling clouds and jagged rocks, evoking feelings of despair and turmoil. Images of suffering bodies conveyed a sense of agony, all overseen by a large, winged creature. A quote on his left peck read, "The path to Paradise begins in Hell."

His strong arms wrapped around her waist, locking her in place, her hands trapped against his chest, which was sticky with sweat. "Hey there, pretty thing." She looked up into the face that was identical to Declan's. "I'm Dempsey. Glad to finally meet you."

The door behind her swung open, and Declan's voice, thick and possessive, filled the hall. "Back away from my fiancée, Demp."

DECLAN SWORE HE could paint the hallway red, or green, depending on how you looked at it. As he took in the scene before him.

He rushed out of the bathroom, barely remembering to grab a towel to cover himself. Stepping into the bathroom, he found Willa wasn't there. He swore he had seen her at the door when he stepped out of the shower. He had forgotten to push the bathroom door closed, knowing if he didn't, it would slowly creep open. A detail he failed to mention to her.

All day, he had struggled to keep himself in check, wanting to reach over and play with her while they were flying, or drag her to the airport bathroom as soon as they landed, and fuck her over the sink. *Why* he was so horny, he couldn't say, but Willa had been wound so tight the closer they got to visiting his family that he knew she needed a release. Knew he needed his own, if he had his way, that release would have been while buried deep inside her.

Instead, he found himself reaching for his cock in the shower, wanting a release on his own, as his earlier fantasies flew through his mind.

He wasn't planning on taking her to bed for the first time in his parents' home. Not when they needed to stay quiet. He needed her to be able to scream his name as he sent her over the edge, to be able to take his time with her without fear of interruption. Despite the orgasm of his own, he found himself still *wanting*. He knew deep down that he wouldn't be able to sleep in the same room with her without something happening.

He was determined to solidify their relationship. To show her that this was it. For both of them. They were already married. It went beyond a drunken mistake for him.

Declan knew Willa wouldn't get that far when he had just seen her at the door, but what he didn't expect was her wrapped in his older brother's arms. Nor did he expect the anger that was coursing through his body at the sight of the two of them.

"Dec. Welcome home," Dempsey smirked, his eyes so much like Declan's, swimming with amusement. The fucker knew what he was doing. "Is she your wife or your fiancée? I just need a refresher on that."

"You know exactly what she is, and you are *not* going to tell Mom and Dad."

"Mmm...Testy." Dempsey tsked.

He couldn't help but roll his eyes like an angsty teenager as he reached for Willa's hand, pulling her into his arms, noting her heart was racing.

Dempsey chuckled and dragged his blue eyes to Willa. He winked at her. "I look forward to getting to know you," he said before he sauntered off to his room down the hall.

Declan pulled Willa into his room, shutting—and locking—the door behind him. He felt like a fucking caveman by doing it, but he needed her away from his brother. Needed her alone, where she was *his*. He crossed his arms as he turned to her, seeing she was mirroring him, standing in the center of the room. Even with the frustration growing, he couldn't help but smirk.

"What the hell was that about, Dec?" Her frustration rolled off of her in waves.

"I didn't like his hands on you," he ground out.

God, did he hate seeing his brother's hands wrapped around his woman. "You're fucking *mine*."

He watched the frustration turn to anger on her face. "Declan, we're *married*. There's no need to get all territorial because of your brother."

"He won't put his hands on you again. Got it?" He swore his blood was boiling. "Or he will no longer *have* hands."

Willa stared at him for a moment. "You're being ridiculous." She crossed her arms. "He caught me when I bumped into him when I was running out of the room."

He cocked an eyebrow at her. "Why were you in such a hurry to leave the room then?" Maybe he hadn't imagined her watching him.

She opened her mouth to answer but shut it, clearly at odds with what she wanted to say.

Smirking, he closed the distance between them, the fight between them not important to him now. Her eyes widened as he caged her in against his desk, pressing a hand weakly against his chest in response.

"Why were you in such a hurry, Willa?" *Say the words*. She shook her head, refusing to take the bait. He cocked his head slightly. "Because if I had to guess, I'd say it was because you got caught spying on me getting out of the shower."

"Only in your dreams would I spy on you in the shower. It's probably some sick fantasy of yours." She quipped, her voice slightly shaky.

He invaded her space, desperately wanting to close the gap, to pull her luscious bottom lip between his lips and devour. To show her who was in control when it came to them. Her eyes fluttered closed, and he *swore* she leaned in a fraction.

Lacking any more self-control, he leaned in, her minty breath filling his senses. "What do you do to me?" He muttered, not missing how her breath hitched.

He felt the pull to her, the mutual need to finally finish what they started three years ago, but a little voice in his head was screaming at him to wait. He was tired of waiting. He was ready to claim, to memorize, every inch of her.

He couldn't wait any longer. He needed to show her how he felt about her. He leaned in, his lips hovering just a breath away from hers.

"Dec? Willa? How many burgers do you want?" Norah's voice came through the door, dampening the rising tension.

"Two for each of us, please." He called out, his voice husky—God, he hoped his mom didn't pick up on that—before he dropped his forehead to Willa's in defeat.

Chapter Fourteen

CONVERSATION HELD UP so well during dinner, Willa hardly had a moment to think about what had happened in Declan's room, despite her desperate need to dissect the whole thing. She had never known him to be jealous, so to find herself being pulled against him out of jealousy was a shock to her system, and maybe even turned her on a little—if she were being honest with herself.

During dinner, she finally met Declan's youngest sibling, Talia, who was in her first year of her master's program to earn her t-DPT, transitional Doctor of Physical Therapy degree *for us lesser folk*, Declan had muttered when Talia threw out the acronym. A smile tugged at her lips as his sister talked, clearly passionate about her schooling and her future goals.

She learned that Dempsey, the eldest Hawke sibling, was an undergrad literature professor at Fairport University. She asked him about the tattoo that she saw on his chest earlier, not missing the glint in his eye when the incident crossed his mind as well. When she asked him what authors they covered in his class, he spoke of Dante, Edgar Allan Poe, Sophocles, and Chaucer. His blue eyes danced with passion as he spoke, eliciting groans from his siblings as if once he got started, he wouldn't stop for a while.

Willa was amazed that someone could feel so passionately about stories others had written. She loved a good book but found herself grabbing spicy romances over The Canterbury Tales. When Declan made that comment to his brother, Dempsey couldn't help but let out a bark of laughter.

She had spent time getting to know them in the group chat they added her to, but it wasn't the same. Texting was just quick responses, dogging on each other, while dinner was an opportunity to get to know each of them better. She loved it, loved getting to know them more.

They questioned her about her interests, what she did in the Air Force, and why she chose that branch over the others. What it was like growing up as an only child. She saw genuine interest on their faces, and that made her feel good, and maybe a touch overwhelmed. They *wanted* to get to know her, the person who was a part of the family already—even if there was a possibility that it wasn't genuine or would last.

She felt a wave of nausea at the thought.

After polishing off her second burger, the damn things were the best she had ever had, Norah cleared her throat, readying herself to say the words Willa had been dreading all night.

"So, Willa," Norah started. "Why didn't you make Declan court you a while before he proposed? I would've made him grovel."

The question wasn't unexpected. She knew it was coming eventually, so why did she freeze?

No one in their right mind just gets engaged without dating first.

No one in their right mind elopes without dating first, either…

The less lying, the better.

She grabbed her tea and took a quick drink to compose herself. "I've been in love with him for years, and so I didn't even question it."

Willa looked around the table and saw all eyes on her. "Our feelings for one another have always been apparent, have they not?"

"That is true," Dempsey said. "We *did* tease Declan about how much he talked about you. I think that was within the first six months of you two meeting."

She looked at Declan. She never heard that story. "Oh? When was this?"

Declan smiled at her as he leaned in to wrap his arm around her shoulder. "When you hurt your ankle."

"That long?"

He shrugged. "When you know, you know."

"That's right," Norah agreed. "It has been a long time coming."

"The timing was always wrong," Declan said.

Willa's heartbeat jumped at the reality of their words.

They were a long time coming, and now she had him. She just needed to convince him that this could be real.

"I think it's sweet," Talia said, sending a smile towards them, playing along. "You've been friends for almost eight years, right?" Willa nodded. "What's a better love story of two friends whose love changes from platonic to romantic?"

"Honestly, the timeline part shouldn't even matter," Dempsey added. Willa heard a little heat behind the words and wondered if that was normal.

Talia looked at him, surprised. "Why Dempsey Hawke, are you finally softening up that cold heart?"

He glared at her as he muttered, "Nothing is softening anywhere."

"I'm sorry I jumped at getting you two here quickly. I guess I hadn't realized you weren't given much time to celebrate." Norah said, guilt in her voice.

"Don't worry about it," Willa said. "Dec and I have all the time in the world to celebrate. Don't we, *Cazzo Piccolo*."

She turned her attention to Declan, patted his cheek with a smile. He sent her a wicked smile before he closed the distance between them, pressed his lips to the spot just in front of her ear. "You'll pay for that." He whispered.

She couldn't hold back the sudden giggle that bubbled up. A year into their friendship, they had decided to take foreign language classes so when they'd travel internationally, they'd be able to say some things in the native language. Willa had taken it upon herself to learn how to say *little dick* in Italian just to tease Declan. She rarely used the nickname, and after their incident a few years ago, she knew it was far from the truth.

Norah set her glass down. "What does that mean? *Cazzo Piccolo*?"

Willa looked from Dec's humor-filled expression

around the table to Norah again. She caught the look on Dempsey's face and knew in that moment he understood what she had said.

"It means—" *Fuck.* What was she going to tell them? Certainly not the truth. "Love of my life. Because that's just what he is."

Norah clasped her hands over her heart as she cooed. "I absolutely love that." She reached for Connor's hand, squeezed. "I'm going to start calling you that, dear. *Cazzo Piccolo.*"

Dempsey looked at Willa, a smile on his face. "Parker would've fucking loved you, Willa."

Parker? What did he have to do with this? She really needed to understand who he was; she felt like she was missing out on an inside joke.

He let out a holler before he stood, grabbed his plate, and then sauntered inside, his entire body shaking from the laughter he was desperately trying to contain.

AS SHE STEPPED into the shower later that night, she thought about how they managed to keep the conversation flowing for hours on end.

She truly loved that, though. She was a talker; she could admit that, but she could also admit that it felt like a major flaw of hers, always afraid of talking too much. Of giving away too much information about herself. She tried her hardest to keep the talking to a minimum whenever she could. Except for Declan, Sofia, and Cruz, she thought she did a rather decent job of it. Being around Declan's family, of being welcomed to talk the way she did—she felt welcome. Not that she had ever felt anything but.

In the past, whenever Norah and Connor would visit Declan, they'd invite her out to lunch. She never turned down the opportunity, but it was a different ballgame talking to them as they were the parents of her best friend, versus the parents of your fiancée—well, husband. Then add in Talia and Dempsey to the mix, and she was happily a part of five different conversations at once.

She dropped her head back, letting the hot water run down her neck before she grabbed her shampoo and got to work on washing away the travel of the day.

Had she really been in North Carolina just this morning? Today had been such a fulfilling day, she could have sworn that a week had passed by. She couldn't wait to meet Declan's other siblings and see how the family dynamic worked. The family she was now a part of.

The thought gave her goosebumps.

As she lathered her skin with soap, the gentle scent of peaches mingled with steam from the hot water, enveloping her in a sweet, fruity aroma that always made her feel relaxed and content.

Rinsing off the soap, she was lost in thoughts about what family get-togethers were like with the Hawke family. Do Norah and her daughters do all the prepping and cooking, while the men hang out in the living room watching whatever sport was on TV? Did the roles get reversed now that the children were older? She smiled to herself as she wondered if Connor walked into the kitchen to steal a kiss from his wife or pull her into a dance while she was covered in food.

With a sigh, she turned off the water, grabbed the cotton towel she had placed on a hook next to the shower.

As she dried herself off, she wondered how she would fit into their dynamic. Her mind drifted to sitting on Declan's lap during a football game, cheering and dropping a kiss on his lips whenever their team scored a touchdown. She imagined herself playfully arguing with Connor and Dempsey over unfair calls, or standing in the kitchen with Norah and Talia, finally learning how to bake a pie.

She reached for her lotion and began to massage it into her arms, imagining the feeling of snuggling on the outdoor couch with Dec and their children, as they watched the Fourth of July fireworks Dempsey had bragged about tonight.

Willa slipped on the ribbed mauve shorts and matching camisole she picked out for sleeping in, before moving on to brush her hair. She sighed when she caught the gleam in her eye.

She had been so caught up in a fantasy, imagining a life with Declan if she could just muster the courage to confess her true feelings to him—and those feelings being reciprocated. But deep down, she knew it was just a pipe dream. The truth was the likelihood of Declan feeling the same way about her was practically nonexistent. He was just a friend to her, nothing more and nothing less. They just had a drunken mistake that would most likely be annulled when they returned home. That their almost kiss was just a heat of the moment, and he had probably not even thought about it since they left his room. Even if it played on repeat in her own mind.

Shaking her head, she hung her towel back up and paused at the door. Taking a deep breath, knowing Declan was waiting for her on the other side, had her stomach knotting with nerves.

DECLAN SET HIS phone down on the table beside him when he heard the shower turn off. He wanted to clear the air on what happened earlier—first with Dempsey, then about that almost kiss.

He found himself replaying their evening, marveling at how she seamlessly transitioned from one conversation to the next. It was one thing he adored about her—the ability to keep up, smoothly switching from one topic to another without missing a beat.

A very large part of him longed to spend future holidays here with her and his family for the next fifty or sixty years. He envisioned having a big wedding in his parents' backyard, against the backdrop of the Rocky Mountains, surrounded by loved ones. He yearned for a long weekend here with her, pregnant with their first child, while his mom taught her the secrets of the Hawke family. His heart ached to settle down here with Willa, forging a new life together after separating from the military.

But as much as he wanted all of that, he needed to make her fall in love with him, prove to her that they were meant to be together, and keep this marriage from dissipating. To turn those words, she had spoken about being in love at dinner, into a reality.

The bathroom door opened, and he watched as she stood there in her pajamas, biting her lip. It was apparent that she was nervous. They had no problem sharing a bed—had done it plenty of times before—so he didn't understand why she'd be nervous.

Declan patted the bed beside him, encouraging her to join him. She waited before walking to him, obviously aware of his eyes on her. When she climbed into bed, she covered herself up, holding the blanket up to her chest.

He cocked an eyebrow at her. She was acting strange, and he found it oddly entertaining.

"Why are you acting strange, Willa?" he asked, finally breaking the silence. "We've shared a bed before."

"I also wasn't irritated with you then." She rebutted.

He turned to her slightly. "You're irritated with me?"

She looked at him and rolled her eyes. "Do you not remember going all caveman because I ran into your brother?"

"Oh, I remember. Seeing my *wife* in my brother's arms will forever be burned in my brain."

"Dec—"

He cut her off, "If anyone is irritated, it should be me. *Cazzo Piccolo.* Really?"

She let out a laugh; the sound warmed his heart. "I couldn't help it." Declan adjusted himself to face her more, as he reached out to tickle her hips. Her eyes widened when she realized what he was doing. "Dec. No. I swear to God. Don't."

"Don't what?" he asked as he playfully dragged his fingers across her hips, eliciting a laugh out of her. "I think you deserve it, la mia dolce figa."

He watched her eyes go from confusion to recognition. "Declan!"

Smiling, he started tickling her again, until she was laughing uncontrollably, face red with laughter. She finally managed to tap his arm twice, telling him she had given up. He rested his hands on her hips, waited until her humor-filled eyes locked onto his.

At that moment, Declan vowed to do whatever it took to keep her this happy until his dying breath.

Chapter Fifteen

WILLA WOKE UP with her back pressed against Declan's chest, his arm slung over her waist, pulling her tight against him.

The awkwardness of getting into bed last night had been diminished when he *insisted* on tickling her as payback. They had fallen asleep comfortably, after laughing over Norah calling Connor, *Cazzo Piccolo*, and discussing their plans on getting through the next two weeks. They knew the questions on when they went from friends to lovers were going to happen, but Willa hated that she had felt caught off guard, or the panic that had risen in her chest before she answered.

Sometime in the night, Declan must have reached for her, pulling her in. How many times had she woken up like this, wrapped in his arms? She dreamed of falling asleep talking about the mundane of life, to wake up with his addictive aroma curled around her in greeting, of wanting this kind of life with him, growing old together.

Not ready to get up or wake him, Willa relaxed her body in his embrace as she gazed through the small gap in the curtain. She couldn't see much, but she was able to catch the sun ascending over the mountains, enveloping them in a mystic glow.

She could see it, the life they could build together. The long weekends they would take to visit the family, or their children running around in the backyard chasing their grandfather and uncles. She heard the laughter bellowing out into the open air when Connor would let one of the little ones jump on him as he feigned surrender. She saw herself round with another child, sitting by a fire with Declan by her side.

As her mind raced with this dream life she so desperately wanted, she decided this was it. This would have to be *the* trip.

They were already married. What harm would it do to convince him?

It was all or nothing.

She was tired of finding other men that would never amount to Declan Hawke. No one would ever make her heart race with a smile. She didn't want to just stay friends with him, damn it. She wanted to be his wife and ride off into the sunset with him. She couldn't bear the thought of them ending the marriage. Losing him because of it. She knew that loss would no doubt throw her into a depression worse than what she had from Cooper.

She couldn't bring herself to settle for anything less than the comfort of his arms. They fit too well together to continue to deny her feelings for him.

As she was lost in her thoughts, she must have shifted, and suddenly she could feel the heavy length that was pure Declan pushed against her ass. His strong presence enveloped her as he nuzzled into her neck and pulled her closer.

His voice sent a shiver of need down her spine to

pool between her thighs as his voice, husky from sleep, whispered, "I want you."

Her heart raced with uncertainty as she struggled to decide what to do. She debated waking him, the thought of him dreaming about another woman tormented her. Was he dreaming of the next person he'd no doubt take to bed when this ordeal was over?

As she lay there contemplating what to do, her thoughts were interrupted by the feeling of him rolling his hips, grinding against her. She *swore* she heard him mutter *Willa,* the thought making her heart skip a beat.

Could he really be dreaming of *her*? That he was thinking about her, even in his sleep? The questions swirled in her mind, leaving her even more uncertain about what to do. Should she wake him and confront him about it, or let him sleep and hold onto the hope that he truly did utter her name?

She wanted to know the truth, but at the same time, she was afraid. The fear of being hurt or disappointed by his actions loomed over her.

She wanted to believe that he did call out her name. If that made her delusional, so be it. She'd wait until he woke up, and then they were going to have a serious conversation. Until then, she would let herself have this moment, this fantasy that *it* had been her name on his lips.

A MOAN ESCAPED her lips. Her body—so soft, so feminine—arched into him as his fingers roamed, sliding over her breasts, her nipples hardened under his touch through the cotton of her top.

Why was she still wearing clothes, he wondered, as his hand trailed down her stomach, where the top had slid up while she slept. She shivered as his fingers brushed over the exposed skin of her hip. He paused briefly at the top of her shorts and waited for a sign—a word, a sound, a gesture—to let him know it was okay. She shifted and leaned into his touch, giving him the permission he needed to continue.

His touch was gentle and deliberate as he slid his hand just inside her waistband. There was one place he wanted to be and could practically *feel* the heat radiating from her, even from her side. He drew his fingers closer to where they wanted to be when her body jolted, her ass jerking into his cock, and a laugh bubbled out of her.

He smiled to himself, knowing Willa was the only person he had ever met who had a ticklish spot on the front of her hip.

Realization dawned on him then. *Willa.* Holy shit. His hand was in her shorts. What was he going to do? As much as he craved to continue, to finally make Willa his, now wasn't the time. Not when he was half asleep. But he couldn't just pull his hand out, not if she was awake.

He kept his hand where it was, as he figured out how to get out of this situation.

Shit, shit, shit.

She rotated slightly towards him, his hand sliding further across her leg, closer to the heat between her thighs. He knew she'd feel suffocatingly tight if he ever got the chance to take her. He felt his cock growing even harder and had to force the thoughts away before all logic went out the window.

She turned her head towards him, eyes closed, a small smile on her face. *She was beautiful, even in sleep,* he thought, slowly pulling his hand up, away from where he wanted to be.

He watched as she opened her eyes. Watched as she processed where she was, and what his hand was doing. She jerked when his hand brushed over that spot on her hip again.

The awareness crossed her face a moment before she jolted, sitting upright. Declan let out a breath when he was able to slip his hand out of her shorts in the movement.

Shifting, he rotated to his back, pulling an arm behind his head to rest on, the other remained on Willa's side of the bed. Craving to touch her again, he gripped the sheet instead, not fully trusting himself.

"I had the weirdest dream."

He cleared his throat, "What about?"

Willa stayed silent and shook her head. "I didn't realize I had fallen asleep." She mumbled. Declan said nothing, waiting to see if she would continue. Eventually, she turned her attention to him. "I—can we talk about something?"

Fuck me.

"Listen, I'm sorry for my hand. You can't control what you do in your sleep."

She blinked at him. *Shit.*

"That's…not what I wanted to talk about. But save that conversation for later." She said with a hint of amusement.

"Oh. What did you want to talk about?"

He studied her face as he waited. Watched the different emotions, the internal battle she was fighting, cross her face.

"Do you think," she paused, "do you wonder how this is going to affect our friendship in the future?"

"This, as in faking an engagement, or eloping?"

"Both?" She said after a moment. *You are mine, so it doesn't matter.*

"I assume we'll come out of it the way we do everything else." What was she getting at?

"You don't think this is going to affect us?" he flinched a little at the hint of worry in her voice.

Absent-mindedly, he lifted his hand and rubbed circles on her back. "Not at all. We've survived deployments and your bastard ex. We can survive this."

She muttered something under her breath, but he didn't catch what.

"I have six months before my contract ends," she said, looking at her lap, fiddling with the ring on her finger.

What in the world? "Willa, what is wrong?" He sat up

and turned them both so they could face one another. "You're worried about our friendship. Your contract? Clearly, something is bothering you. If you separate, I'll always be with you. No matter what happens between us."

She looked at him, her green eyes glossy with tears. "Do you even want to be married?"

Declan cupped her cheeks and kissed her forehead. "Willa, are you okay?" He should tell her right now, ease her fears. But something stopped him, fearing that this was her rejection or something else. He wasn't sure.

"I really love your family, Dec."

"I—Willa, what is going on?"

"Do you think we're going to disappoint them? When they learn the truth?"

Is that what has been bothering her? She's worried about their opinion of her, if they told them the full truth?

"Willa, they love you. Married or not. It doesn't matter. Not to them. When all of this is over, I will take full responsibility. I'm the one who put us in this situation, not you."

"But I'm going along with it."

"It's not like I murdered someone and you're my accomplice." She scoffed. "I'm serious, Willa. No matter what happens after this trip, they will always love you. They already see you as family."

She hiccupped at his words. "Which gives them all the more reason to hate me." Dropping her head in her hands, she leaned forward when Declan wrapped his arms around her.

He ran his hands up and down her back, feeling the

tension in her muscles. He couldn't help but wonder the same thing—how would his family take it when he told them the truth about his relationship with her? Declan knew the answer they'd accept. Understanding would come later. He couldn't bear the thought of disappointing his family.

But what about Willa? He wanted her, wanted to spend whatever time he had left on earth to prove to her that they were meant for each other, that he wanted this marriage to work as if it were his next breath. He wanted her to see that they could make it work, that the love they shared was worth fighting for.

A soft knock on the door had both of them jumping.

"Yes?" Dec called out, his arms wrapping around Willa to prevent her from leaving. He wasn't ready to let her go just yet.

The door opened; Talia's long brown hair pulled back into a French braid. "Sorry to interrupt," she stepped just inside the room, dressed in a navy blue floral t-shirt and denim capris. "But I wanted to see if I could steal Willa away for a few hours to go to brunch. I have to head back to school tonight and won't be able to make it back until next week, before you guys leave."

Declan pressed his lips to Willa's temple before he dropped his arms. "I think that sounds like a great idea."

Willa wiped at her eyes, wanting to erase the tears that lingered on her cheeks. Talia's blue eyes widened. "Oh, I'm sorry! If you're not up for it, we can totally reschedule!"

"It's fine. I just had a bad dream." Willa said,

smiling at Talia. "Give me about twenty minutes, and I can be ready if that's okay with you?"

Talia beamed, "That's perfect. I'll meet you downstairs!"

WHEN DECLAN COULDN'T find anyone else, he decided to lie outside on one of the dark blue couches, thinking over his plans to get Willa to see that they were meant to be together. He slid his sunglasses on as the sun loomed higher into the sky.

He stared at the mountains when a door opened behind him. Dempsey dropped onto the couch beside Declan.

"Morning. No *fiancée*?" Dempsey asked, sipping his coffee.

"Brunch with Talia." Declan sat up and faced his brother.

"I know we've gotten to know her through the chat, but she really is great, Dec. I can see why you're so stuck on her.

Declan studied his older brother. His brown hair, unruly from sleep, always had a slight curl to it, and in recent years had learned to embrace it.

It looked good on him, he thought, and was sure that the combination of tattoos and unkempt hair attracted an ungodly amount of women.

"She is."

Dempsey took another sip of his coffee before setting it down on the table in front of him. "Took you way too long to finally bag her, though. Closing in on eight years, right?"

Declan rolled his eyes, fighting the urge to push his brother. "You're not allowed to give me shit until you've found the woman of your dreams and you're in my position," Dempsey said nothing, his jaw tightening as he avoided eye contact. "Holy shit. You have, haven't you?"

Dempsey's eyes shifted to Declan; the usually bright blue darkened. "It's—I don't know."

Dec lifted an eyebrow. *Oh, he's got it bad.* "What's bugging you about her?"

He waited. He could be patient; it was a part of his job, and he knew that eventually, whatever was bothering his older brother would make him snap. Just how long would it take?

Dempsey dragged a hand through his hair before he sighed. "I can't get enough of her. There's just something about her that gets under my skin. It's not just her beauty or her intelligence—and God is she the smartest woman I've ever met—it's the way she carries herself, with an air of confidence and a hint of mystery. Every time I see her, I find myself drawn to her like a moth to a flame. I *know* that being around her is a bad idea, but I can't seem to stay away. It's like she has some kind of magnetic pull on me, and I'm powerless to resist." Declan sat back and crossed his arms as Dempsey spoke. "She's an enigma, and it drives me crazy. I want to know everything about her—what makes her tick, what she's thinking, what she's feeling. She tries keeping me at arm's length, but she struggles. I know she wants to let me in, but I know that she's hesitant, too. She's warm and affectionate, but she can also be cold and distant in the blink of an eye, like she realizes what is going on." Declan had never recalled seeing his brother so *untethered*. Dempsey was calm and collected. The brother that sat next to him was a damn mess.

Dempsey paused, reflecting. "I know that being around her is dangerous, but I can't help but be intrigued by her. I want to unravel everything about her, to delve deep into the complexities of her mind. And I know that this fascination—this *obsession*—will be my downfall if I'm not careful. But I can't seem to stop myself from falling deeper and deeper into her enigmatic allure, and I don't know what to do about it." *That's because big brother, you found your other half, the storm you can't weather.*

Declan smiled at his brother. Dempsey had no clue that he was already deeply in love with whoever this woman was.

Dempsey looked at him, scowled. "Why are you smiling?"

He patted his brother on the shoulder. "You'll figure it out one day."

Chapter Sixteen

WILLA HANDED THE waitress her menu before grabbing her tea, savoring the sweetness of the strawberry mixed in. The drive to Rise and Grind was smooth, filled with casual conversation about the city the Hawkes lived in.

She was grateful that she didn't feel uncomfortable being alone with Talia. They got along well enough that there was no need for awkwardness. Talia was charismatic and witty, able to hold a conversation about anything. Willa enjoyed the easy-going and enjoyable company that Talia provided.

"So," Talia started. "I just want to say that for the last seven years, Declan has talked about you nonstop, and I'm glad that he finally grew the balls to make his move. Even if you did go from zero to sixty."

Curiosity piqued; Willa sat forward. "Talked about me nonstop?"

Talia grabbed her mimosa and took a drink. "Girl, he has been in love with you for *years*. He talks about you every chance he can. It'll sound creepy, but we know a lot about you. You've been one of us for years. Outside the group chat, I guess."

Willa grabbed her drink and swallowed half of it

before she spoke. "Did he tell you about the depression?"

Talia's face softened. "He did, vaguely." She added quickly. "When we first started hearing about you, he mentioned it but didn't elaborate. Not his story to tell, you know?"

She nodded. "I went through a horrible breakup. We were together for years, planned out our entire future together."

"What happened?"

"He was on board with me joining the Air Force, then decided he couldn't handle the long-distance relationship, nor did he want to uproot his life to follow me wherever I was sent. Even though he was on board the entire fucking time." She was still *so* pissed about Cooper for everything. She felt like she had lost a solid year of her life, grieving the relationship, the life she thought she was going to have with him, and the depression.

She locked eyes with their waitress and pointed to Talia's glass. She needed a drink. A mimosa wasn't going to be strong enough, but it was a start.

Talia reached for her hand and squeezed once before she let go. "I understand, and I'm sorry you've had to go through this. I have an ex, he's—" she trailed off.

"You don't have to talk about it," Willa said. "I know what it's like."

"No, you're fine. It's still pretty fresh, and I really don't know how to feel still."

"Did you love him?"

She nodded. "I did. Or—do. He's the reason I'm becoming a physical therapist."

"Really?" Willa asked. She wouldn't have assumed, not with the way Talia lit up when she talked about her career.

"Yep. I love it, don't get me wrong, and I'm excited to see what I can do with my career. I want to work with the Salt Lake Sirens. It's been a goal of mine since I was in high school." She didn't know much about the field, but she assumed that to get assigned to a major team like the Sirens, it would be competitive. Though with the way Talia talked about her career, she didn't doubt her for a second.

"What are the chances you can get a job with them when you graduate?" Willa sat back and smiled at the waitress as she dropped off two more mimosas and their meals. The smell of the smoked bacon she ordered made her mouth water. "Thank you."

Talia dug into her French toast before she spoke. "Depends on how I do in school. Which I'm top of my class if I'm allowed to brag."

"Always are," Willa commented.

"I knew I liked you." Talia gestured with her fork. "I have three years to get my t-DPT. I'm hoping to do it in two since I don't want to take summers off. I do know the current therapist, thanks to Dad, and he wants to retire soon. Three more seasons is what he told me when I saw him a few weeks ago. Excluding the season that's wrapping up now. If things go my way, I graduate a year early, and he can put in a good word for me to get a position under him, and learn the ropes of how they operate. Be under his wing for a year before he's done."

"Sounds like a win-win situation to me," Willa said as she put another forkful of pancakes in her mouth.

"That's exactly my thought. Zayne, my ex, is the catcher for the team. This is—"

"Talia?" A deep voice came from behind Willa. She watched Talia's eyes widen before she turned to see the tall man walking their way.

His sun-kissed, tawny skin reflected the hours he had spent in the sun, giving him a bronzed glow. As he approached, his captivating smile illuminated his handsome face, framed by dark chocolate-colored hair peeking out from under a well-worn SLS baseball cap.

"Fuck me," Talia muttered under her breath. "This is him."

His eyes sparkled as he stopped at their table, holding his arms out to envelop Talia in a hug, who folded into him with ease. But Willa could see it, those tiny cracks in Talia as she was held by Zayne.

"Zayne, how are you?" Talia asked, her voice void of emotion.

To love someone who you were no longer with, needing to put a brave face on for. Willa's heart ached for Talia.

They broke their hug before turning towards Willa, who stood out of politeness.

"Willa, this is Zayne," Talia said. "Zayne, this is Willa."

He smiled at Willa, holding out a hand to her. When she slid her hand in his, she felt the calluses on his palm. He gripped her hand, kept her from pulling away. She didn't like that, the forced connection. It made her want to pull away even more.

"Willa, as in Dec's Willa?" He asked, looking between the two women. He pressed a kiss to her hand, no doubt something he thought women fawned over. "I've heard so much about you. It's nice to meet you."

She smiled at him. "Wish I could say the same."

His smile faltered a little but remained plastered on his face. She didn't mean for it to come off rude, but from the smirk on Talia's face, she wasn't going to regret it.

He released her hand as he slid into the empty chair at their table. Willa heard Talia sigh before they slid into their seats again. Willa couldn't help but curl her lip up at his assumption that he was welcome there.

"How's school going, Tal?" Zayne asked, pulling off his hat, running a hand through his hair.

"It's fine." Talia grabbed her drink and swallowed the remaining contents. "How's the season going?" Willa could tell how oblivious Zayne was to Talia, at how she just wanted him to leave them alone.

"You haven't been watching?" He asked, hurt apparent in his voice.

"I've been busy." She answered quietly. She fidgeted with her fork, spinning it around in the syrup pooled on her plate.

He shifted in his seat and whispered, "I miss you, Tal."

Talia mumbled under her breath as she shoveled more food into her mouth to prevent herself from saying anything she'd regret, avoiding eye contact with both of them.

Willa felt a deep sense of sadness watching them, clearly struggling with their emotions and the tension between them. It was an all-too-familiar feeling for her. She understood the conflicting emotions, the reluctance to face the truth.

After what felt like an eternity, Zayne turned his attention to Willa. "So, are you and Dec finally together? I swear he's been in love with you for as long as Talia and I were together."

Without a trace of guilt, Willa smiled and held up her left hand, showing off the sapphire ring on her finger. "Only a few days, actually."

Zayne grabbed her hand and studied the ring before sending her a smile. "Gorgeous. Suits you perfectly. I can already tell the two of you make a gorgeous couple."

She felt a blush creep on her cheeks. "Thanks."

Talia raised her hand to flag down the waitress. Willa looked at her, and she gestured with two fingers, moving swiftly. She was ready to get out of there.

When the waitress brought the check, Zayne beat Talia to it, covering it with his hand. "I'll take care of this. Consider it my gift to the happy couple." He smiled at Willa before he looked at Talia. "Can we talk? Privately, sometime?"

With how fidgety Talia was, Willa looked at her phone, noted the time. She looked at Talia. "Don't we need to get going?"

Talia nodded, catching on immediately, and swung her bag over her shoulder as she stood. "I—I don't know if that's a good idea, Zayne."

He stood and grabbed her arm. "Please? I'm not okay with how things ended."

Willa watched Talia's eyes fill with tears. "Let me think about it. Please?"

Zayne nodded, then leaned down to kiss her on the cheek. "Call me when you're ready to talk." He grabbed the check and nodded to Willa before he walked away.

"Can we go?" Talia asked Willa. The woman looked torn up. She obviously needed to have a conversation with the man, but to be caught off guard the way she had been—Willa understood. She hoped that they'd get the closure—if that was what they wanted—when she was ready.

"Yeah, of course."

THEY LEFT THE restaurant and walked off some of their brunch, as they explored downtown Bedpa. Willa didn't bring up the conversation with Zayne. She decided to let that be Talia's domain if she decided to talk about it.

They approached a bridal boutique, the stunning dresses in the window catching Willa's eye. A smile spread across her face as she imagined herself in one of those beautiful gowns, walking down the aisle towards the man of her dreams. She couldn't wait for the day she got to plan her wedding; to choose the perfect dress, the flowers. She desperately wanted her plan to work in proving to Declan they were perfect together. If she succeeded, that day may not be far off.

"Come on!" Talia said, pulling Willa with her.

"Wait, what?" Willa said. "We're already… You know."

"And *you* should remember that Declan is the first to get married, and my parents think you're only engaged. Which means, she gestured to the shop. "You have to go dress shopping."

Shit. She was right. Willa groaned at the thought.

Talia pulled her into the store. "It's never too soon to start planning!" She said, waving to the elderly woman by the counter. "Besides, the dresses here are one of a kind. Vivian here designs them all. Don't you, Vivi?"

The elderly woman smiled at Willa; her blue eyes twinkled. She had short, white hair that framed her face in soft waves, and a few scattered age spots on her face. She stood and shuffled over to them. She was on the small side, with a slight stoop that came with age. Vivian wore a pale yellow cardigan with a black skirt, allowing her to move comfortably.

"It's a pleasure to meet you." She said, grabbing Willa's hand in her own delicate ones, prominent veins revealing themselves.

"I'm Willa Evans. It's wonderful to meet you."

Vivian smiled at her before releasing her hand. "I hear you're engaged to our own Declan Hawke. What a good boy he is. You chose well. In husband and family." She added as she wrapped her arms around Talia. "Hello, my dear."

"You can't get much better than the Hawkes," Talia answered. "Is momma here yet?"

Wait, what? "Norah is coming?"

Talia looked at her sheepishly, before the front door flew open, and Norah walked in.

"I'm so sorry I'm late." She said, pushing her sunglasses up on top of her head.

"You planned this?" Willa asked.

"I did," Norah said, hugging Vivian. "I know it's probably too soon, but since you and Dec both live in North Carolina, I wanted an opportunity to do some motherly things with you. No pressure, but I thought it would be fun to have a girls' day—sans Taelyn, unfortunately—and try on dresses. Get a feel for what you'd like to wear."

"Oh, I uhh," *fuck.* "I don't have a whole lot of money saved up right now. I'd hate to find the right dress and not be able to buy it." She needed to get out of this as fast as she possibly could. She really didn't want to do this right now.

Norah patted her on the cheek. "Nonsense. It doesn't hurt to try them on. Let loose for a little while. No purchases. No pressure. I just thought it would be fun."

Willa chewed on her lip, unsure. She really shouldn't go along with this. But the excitement on Norah and Talia's faces… She didn't want to say no and hurt anyone's feelings, but saying yes meant giving in to her delusions. "Okay. Let's try some on."

Cheers rang out as Vivian got to work pulling three dresses from various spots, before pulling Willa into a dressing room.

Willa stripped down to her blush-colored bra and panties and slipped into the first dress when Vivian had it ready for her.

"How long have you known Declan?" She asked, wanting to break the stifling silence.

Vivian hummed as she buttoned the back. "His

entire life. Kat, his Grammy, has been my best friend since we were in diapers."

"That's amazing. To be so close to someone, watching them grow. Their kids."

"And their kids," Vivian smiled. "I hope I get to be around long enough to see one of those kids having babies of their own."

Willa's heart leaped at the thought of having a family with Declan. She could imagine herself cradling a tiny, warm bundle in her arms, feeling the overwhelming love and bright hope for their future. The image of Declan holding their baby, his eyes sparkling with pride and affection, filled her with joy. She could see a home filled with laughter and the sound of little feet running around.

What an amazing life that would be.

"Alright. Now, the rule in my shop is you don't get to see the dress until you are in front of the mirrors in the main room, where Norah and Talia are waiting. Got it?"

Willa blinked at her, not having expected the stern tone she took on. "Yes, ma'am."

"Good. The mirrors have a cover over them. I don't want the bride-to-be taking a peek in the mirror before I'm ready for her to see."

Vivian led the way to a trio of covered mirrors where an elevated platform was placed. While she fussed with the dress, making it perfect, Willa heard Norah and Talia talking. She couldn't hear their conversation; they must've been too far away.

Vivian stepped down, pulling the curtains back.

Willa took in the dress she wore. A bohemian-inspired gown, with flowy layers of chiffon and delicate lace details. She swayed slightly, feeling the dress move with her, creating a dreamy, ethereal effect. The soft, romantic silhouette made her feel like she was floating in the air. She turned slightly to check out the back of the dress, which came to the middle of her back. Although it was beautiful, she couldn't see herself wearing it down the aisle.

Norah smiled at her in the mirror. "It's beautiful, Vivi."

"It is." The elderly woman agreed, clasping her hands together. "But it's not the one."

Norah and Talia shook their heads. "No, it's not."

"Come, Willa. Let's go try on the next one. I try to start simple and work as I learn more about the bride."

She stood in front of the trio of mirrors once again, staring at her reflection. The dress she wore was gorgeous. The way it hugged her curves and the way the fabric flowed as she twirled around. The delicate lace and tulle fabric felt smooth against her skin, and the way the dress flared out at the waist made her feel elegant and graceful. The sweetheart necklace added a touch of regal sophistication.

"This isn't the one." She muttered. She loved it, it was beautiful, but she couldn't see herself in it.

"It looks so good on you, though," Talia commented, her eyes full of stars as she looked at the dress.

"It really is beautiful," Norah added, wiping at her eyes. "Declan would be floored seeing you in this dress."

"I know." She looked at Vivian in the mirror. "You

do such amazing work, Vivian. But it's not it. I can see myself going to a ball in it, but not my wedding."

Vivian said nothing but nodded. "I agree. Let's go try on the next one, then. It's sleeker. Sophisticated. Sexy."

"I'm excited to try it on." Willa felt a weight on her chest as she turned and smiled at Norah and Talia. She was trying to keep her attitude upbeat, but deep down, she wanted to cry. She wanted to tell them that this was all for nothing, that everything was a ruse.

She started walking past the other dresses hanging up, waiting for the day they were picked by a bride, when one in particular caught her eye. "Vivian. Can I try this one on?" Willa didn't know why she was bothering; it wasn't like this was real, but something inside her said, *try it on*. Like she needed to.

Vivian turned and looked at the dress Willa was rubbing her finger over. "Of course. Go on in, and I'll follow you with it."

Inside the dressing room, Willa pulled the zipper down on the princess gown and slipped out of it carefully. She waited for Vivian to be ready before she stepped into the satin dress.

They repeated the steps to the main room and waited for Vivian to fluff out the train before she pulled the curtains back.

Collective gasps filled the room.

The A-line dress was just—stunning. Willa had no other words to describe it. The skirt elegantly flared, with the front skimming the floor and the train billowing behind. Willa shifted slightly, catching sight of the thigh-high slit on her left leg, something she didn't notice walking out of the dressing room. She could already picture Declan's face when he saw how daring the slit was. Running her hand up her leg, she realized how high the slit went, and couldn't help but smile, imagining Declan teasing her all through their reception. Making playful comments about how easy it would be to slide his hand into the slit, taking advantage of her whenever he pleased.

A shiver slid up her spine at the thought.

"Willa," Norah trailed off. They locked eyes and smiled at one another. Norah's eyes were filled with tears. "You look—"

She couldn't help but feel overwhelmed with emotion. The dress was the perfect embodiment of everything she had ever dreamt of for her wedding day. It was as if the gown had been plucked straight from her own imagination.

"Magnificent." Talia finished for her mother, who was busy wiping her eyes with a tissue. "Seriously, Willa."

She studied herself in the mirror, admiring the intricate details of the romantic neckline, highlighting her collarbone, exuding a feminine and delicate aura. The off-shoulder sleeves provided subtle coverage—which would gain approval from her family—while also adding a hint of softness to the dress. Something that she could truly see herself walking down the aisle in, something that would, no doubt, have Declan's knees weakening. Elegant folds of satin sat on the bodice, adding texture and depth, subtly enhancing the bustline, without making her overflow out of the dress.

Willa ran her hands down her sides, where the dress

accentuated her natural curves, creating an elegant hourglass silhouette, admiring herself in the mirror, her eyes glistening with tears.

She could see it now—walking down the aisle in this dress, the tender smile on Declan's face, the way his eyes would light up at the sight of her. She could hear the soft music playing in the background, the sweet scents of flowers that filled the crisp Utah air. She pictured the tears of joy and the overwhelming emotions that would sweep over her as they declared their love in front of everyone they cared about; envisioned the moment they would be pronounced husband and wife and the elation that would fill her heart as they embraced one another for the first time as a married couple.

"Willa?" Norah asked, snapping her back to reality.

"Hmm?" She asked. Had Norah been speaking to her this entire time? "I'm sorry, I didn't hear anything that was said."

Norah smiled at her. "I had asked what you thought of the dress, but now I'm realizing that was silly of me. You look like a dream in this dress."

"I feel like I'm in one," Willa said as she studied herself again. She didn't want to take the dress off. Didn't want to forget this feeling.

She sighed, hoping that the others thought it was done in awe, but who was she kidding? She was going to take this dress off, and that would be that. She needed to tell Declan that she was in love with him, that she wanted to be with him for real, before she could get all starry-eyed when it came to wedding dresses.

Chapter Seventeen

WILLA FELT LIKE she was walking on cloud nine, as they left the bridal boutique. She spent what felt like hours sitting in that dress. She wanted to know what it felt like to walk in it, sit in it, and at one point, she and Talia started dancing just to know what it felt like.

They were walking back to Talia's white Camry when they walked past a clothing store. The A-line ivory dress in the window caught Willa's eye.

"Can we go in? I love that dress." She asked Talia, gesturing to the dress in the window. "Unless you have somewhere to be?"

Talia smiled at her as she headed towards the door. "Absolutely not. If I'm alone right now, I'm going to wallow, and I don't want to do that. Fuck that."

As they walked in, Talia was immediately pulled into a conversation with someone she knew. Not wanting to intrude, Willa quietly made her way toward the dresses. The ivory dress in the window was the exact dress she bought a few years ago that drove Declan crazy. The dress she got *married* in. She had always loved the dress and had been hoping to find it in a different color, but had never been able to locate it, even after hours of searching online.

She struck gold when she found the ivory dress on a colorful rack; the dresses behind it were identical in style and were in a wide variety of colors.

"Hell yes." She muttered to herself.

"You should get the ruby red one," Talia said, making Willa jump.

She looked at Talia, then back at the dresses, and ran her fingers over the baby blue dress she was holding onto.

"Really? I was thinking this one." She pulled the blue dress out to show Talia.

"Trust me. The red will bring that man to his knees." She wiggled her eyebrows before she reached over to grab the red dress, pulling it off the rack.

Willa scrunched her nose. "We're already married."

"So?" She pushed the dress into Willa's hand. "You bagged the man, got the ring. Are you trying to tell me that's that? You need to keep the spice alive."

"Talia!" Willa felt her face reddening. Why was she always making friends with people who knew how to mess with her like this? "Declan is your brother."

"And?" Talia led them to the dressing rooms. "He's a man, they're all the same. Put on some sexy lingerie, put this dress on. Maybe light a few candles. He'll be a goner."

When Willa didn't make an effort to hang up the dresses, Talia smiled at her, took the dresses, and put them on the hooks. "Try them both on. The blue looks amazing, but I can *promise* you that the red will look even better."

She stepped back and slid the curtain closed, leaving

Willa in the small room. On a sigh, she began to undress again, slipped into the blue dress.

Willa studied herself in the mirror. The blue dress complimented her summer tan perfectly as she admired her reflection from all angles in the mirror. Its A-line silhouette was both flattering and feminine, thanks to the fitted bodice and flared skirt that accentuated her waist and gracefully skimmed over her hips. The wrap-around feature added versatility, allowing her to tie it in the front, side, or back. Running her hand over the puffy chiffon sleeve, she appreciated the soft and delicate touch they added to the overall look of the dress.

Talia was wrong about the red—the blue was the perfect color; this was the one she was going to buy. Red wasn't her color; soft colors were. Bold colors scared her if she were being honest.

She slid her gaze to the red dress that hung on the wall. Guilt formed in her chest as she pulled her jeans back into place. She looked at the red dress again and sighed. She didn't want to ignore Talia's comment. She didn't have to buy the dress, much like the wedding dress, but at least humor her new friend by trying it on.

Pulling off her jeans again, she slid the red dress on. When she turned to the mirror, she let out a gasp. The rich color made her tanned skin glow and brought out the vibrancy of her eyes. She ran her hands across the fabric, feeling the softness against her skin. Despite herself, she smiled.

"Willa, I heard that gasp, and I know you're in the red dress. If you don't show me," Talia trailed off.

Willa did a quick once-over of herself in the dress

before she pulled the curtain back, saw Talia waiting in a plush chair.

"Holy shit, you look even better than I expected."

She stepped out of the room and turned to the mirrors in the main space. Talia jumped out of the chair and came up behind her. "I know you like softer colors, and I'm not saying they don't look good on you, because they do. But red is one hundred percent your color."

"You really think so?" She turned and studied herself in the mirror.

"I do." Talia smiled at Willa in the mirror. "Okay, because I'm a dreamer, picture this. You and Dec are outside, surrounded by candles at sunset. The mountains in the background. Since he's the most romantic of my brothers, he'll pull you into a slow dance. Music or not, you're choice. But in my opinion, slow dancing without music is more intimate."

"I love it when he pulls me into a music-less dance," she muttered to herself, thinking of all the times Declan would walk into her kitchen while she was making them food, pulling her into a slow dance. She'd laugh, see the humor in his eyes, while her heart pounded in her chest at the gesture.

"They're the best," Talia said. "Growing up, he'd pull me into a dance all the time, spinning and twirling me around the living room. My brothers showed me how a man should treat a woman. But I think, because of Declan's willingness to dance with his baby sister, he's the reason why I'm such a hopeless romantic."

The image of a teenage Declan dancing with a five-year-old Talia, spinning around the living room, her laughter filling the room, played in Willa's hand as she made her way to the counter to check out. It made her think of a possible future, of Declan dancing with their own daughter.

"I'll buy the red." She decided from that thought alone. "Actually, I think I'm going to buy both. He's not going to know what hit him."

"Atta girl," Talia said, beaming.

She let out a dreamy sigh as she swiped her credit card.

DECLAN, STILL SOAKING up the sun outside, saw his mom rush inside with a white garment bag. She locked eyes with him quickly before she turned towards the stairs.

"Mom, do you need help?" He asked as he got up and headed back inside.

She looked at him, a little flushed. "Oh no. I got it."

He stopped at the bottom of the stairs. "You're struggling. What is that? Or should I ask *who* is that?"

Norah's blue eyes bore into his before she rolled them. "If you keep asking me questions, it's going to be you."

He laughed and followed his mother up the stairs, making sure she didn't fall. "Funny. But seriously—"

"Talia and I introduced Willa to Vivi." Norah reached the top step and turned towards her room.

"Vivi," he muttered before realization struck him. "Mom. What did you do?"

When she didn't respond, he followed her into her room. He smiled to himself when he took in the familiar room. The walls were still a calming pale green, giving off a soft and peaceful atmosphere. Declan wandered towards the oak bed frame that they've had since before he was born, with its plush pillows and cozy duvet. The room gave him a sense of nostalgia. He loved that his parents never changed their room, except for a few changes here and there. He heard Norah shuffling around in her closet, obviously trying to make room for whatever she had in the white garment bag. He glanced towards the closet, debating on whether he wanted to go in and help or let her handle it.

Deciding on the latter, he made his way to the bed and settled on it. While he waited, he took in the framed photographs adorning the walls, each one capturing precious family memories from vacations and special moments. The gentle breeze from the open windows caused the sheer curtains to flutter. He shifted his focus to the windows, taking in the familiar scent of home and the sight of houseplants basking in the sunlight on the windowsill.

"Mom." She popped her head out of her closet and smiled innocently at him.

"What?"

He groaned. "You know what. Why did you take Willa to Vivi's?"

She shrugged. "Why wouldn't I want her to meet

Vivi? She's as much your grandmother as Kit Kat is. I simply wanted her to meet the woman you're marrying."

"So, you could've planned a lunch or dinner where we could go to Vivi's house. But you took Willa to Vivi's store."

"Boutique." Norah corrected. Declan rolled his eyes. "Don't sass me, Declan Matthew."

"Mom," he whined as he sat down on her bed. Why did she have to be like this? He knew it was going to happen, *especially* because neither Taelyn nor Talia were anywhere near getting married. But he wanted to be able to warn Willa about it. He knew she was going to give him an earful when she got home.

Norah sat down next to him and patted his hand twice before she gripped it. "I can't wait for you to see her, Dec. She only tried on three in total. She looked gorgeous in all three of them."

"She looks gorgeous in everything," he muttered, thinking about how she looked in that ivory dress when they eloped.

"That she does, but you should've seen how she *glowed* in that final dress. I know she was just humoring me, but she said she'd try them on, have a little fun. I couldn't resist buying it for her."

"You didn't have to buy her a wedding dress." This was not going to go over well with Willa. "We can take care of our own wedding, Mom."

"I know you can, and I trust that you will for everything else, but I couldn't let this dress go to someone else, Dec."

He nodded, not knowing what else he could say. He

was going to have to go downtown and pay Vivi the money for the dress. He couldn't have his parents paying for it when he wasn't even sure where they stood.

"Your heart is going to melt when you see her," Norah added. "Have you guys given any thought to where the wedding will happen? Would her family be okay to travel?"

He dragged a hand through his hair. "Ahh, it's just her dad. He lives in Indiana."

"Her mom? Siblings?"

"Just her and her dad. Her mom abandoned them when she was a child."

"Oh no, that's awful. No contact?"

"Nope." He sighed. "Henry is nice, he's just very… impersonal."

He thought about the only time he had met Henry Evans. He was friendly but didn't engage in conversation unless it was directed at him.

"I'm sorry to hear that. Hopefully, this trip doesn't scare Willa out of the wedding since we can be a bit much when everyone is home."

"Is Taelyn coming home?"

Norah nodded. "She is. She's globe-trotting again and said she'll be home by my birthday. Delaney will be here on Wednesday."

He felt the excitement bubble up in his chest. Having all of his siblings in one place was rare, and he was glad that they were making it happen. He couldn't wait to officially introduce Willa to them.

Chapter Eighteen

WILLA RUSHED INTO the house after getting the green light from Talia. She wanted to hide the red dress from Declan, deciding that she would wear it when she told him her true feelings.

She hurried upstairs, pulled out her suitcase from under the bed, and put the red dress in the bag before sliding the bag back into place. As she stood, Declan walked into the room.

"Hey, I saw Talia downstairs, was wondering where you ran off to. Have a good time?" He smiled at her, completely oblivious to what she had been doing. Relief flooded over her at the realization. Her red dress was still a surprise.

"We did. Went to brunch. Met Talia's ex, then I got ambushed at Vivi's." She set the paper bag on the bed.

"You met Zayne?" Declan asked, sitting on the edge of the bed, blue eyes blazing with anger.

"I did. He's," she paused. How should she describe the man who gave her a weird vibe?

"An asshole is what he is. No point trying to avoid saying it."

"He didn't seem *that* bad. You can tell they still love each other." Willa fiddled with the handle of the bag.

He grunted but didn't say anything. She wanted to press, to learn more about Talia and Zayne's relationship, but knew it wasn't her place.

"What's in the bag?" He asked finally.

"Huh?" She stopped and looked down at the ribbon twisted around her fingers. "Oh."

She smiled at him as she reached into the bag, pulling out the baby blue dress.

"Is that—" his eyes widened as he took in the entire dress. "You found it in another color."

"I did." She held the dress up to her body. His eyes darkened.

"Put it on. Now." He stood and stalked towards her. She failed to suppress the grin that spread over her face as he moved in, pinning her gently between him and the bedside table.

"Dec—" He was in her space; his scent filled her senses. She felt her eyes roll back at the smell. She put a hand on his chest, making any attempt to keep some distance. "I worked up a sweat trying on dresses. I stink. I need to shower; I don't want to get the dress dirty."

She knew she was rambling, but she lost her train of thought as he leaned in and grazed his nose along the sensitive spot under her ear, sending a chill down her spine. She heard the faint sound of him inhaling.

"Dec," her heart was pounding, she couldn't think, couldn't focus. All she could feel were his lips as they traced along her jaw. She was lost in the moment, completely consumed by the sensation of his touch.

His hands were on her waist, and she could feel the heat radiating from his body. The electricity between them was tangible, sparking a fire within her that she was tired of ignoring.

As his lips continued to move along her jaw, she felt her knees grow weak, rendering her powerless to him. She wanted to pull him to her, to take his mouth with hers, to give in to the primal need she felt for him. Every nerve in her body was on edge, aching for more of his touch.

"Willa," he whispered, his breath warm against her skin as he pulled back slightly to look into her eyes, his own full of need, of want. He looked as if he wanted her as bad as she wanted him—*needed* him.

He slammed his lips against hers, his hands gripped her waist tighter, pulling her closer to him. Willa felt a rush of emotions that threatened to overwhelm her at that moment. She felt a sense of surrender in the air. The barriers that they had carefully constructed were beginning to crumble.

With his lips on hers, his tongue pushing into her mouth, she allowed herself to be consumed by the passion that swept through her. She met his urgency with her own, her hands reaching up to tangle in his hair as she pressed herself closer to him. In that moment, nothing else mattered. There was no one else in the world but the two of them, and the fire that blazed between them.

When he finally pulled away, she could see the turmoil of emotions in his eyes. There was a vulnerability there, a rawness that mirrored the feelings that were coursing through her own veins.

"Willa," he whispered again. "I l—"

"Dec!" Talia's voice rang through the closed door.

"I swear, I'm going to kill someone if we get interrupted again." He dropped his forehead against Willa's. She closed her eyes, feelings mutual. "What now, Tal?"

The door opened behind him. Declan shifted and slid his arm over Willa's shoulders, as she wound a hand around his waist and gripped his shirt. Talia smiled at the two of them, raised her eyebrows at Willa, who had the dress still clutched to her chest.

"Sorry to interrupt whatever this," she wiggled her fingers at them. "Is. I was getting ready to head back to school. I have a shift tonight, so I need to head out early."

Willa felt Declan's body relax and released his shirt. He walked over to Talia and pulled her in for a hug. She set the dress down on the bed and walked over to them, being tugged into a hug as soon as Declan released his sister.

"It was so great getting to *finally* meet you," Talia said when she broke apart from Willa. "It's going to be so nice having another girl in the family. It sucks being outnumbered."

Willa let out a laugh. "Happy to help in any way that I can."

"I'll be back next week for Mom's birthday," she told Declan. "Dad said that Del and Taelyn are going to be here too."

"Mom told me just before you guys got back." He said, running a hand through his hair. "Speaking of—did you really ambush Willa into trying on wedding dresses?"

Talia's eyes sparkled with excitement. "Oh, I wish you could've seen Willa in that dress, Dec. She was stunning." She grabbed Willa's hand. "You should've bought it."

Willa flushed. She wished she did. "Hopefully it'll be there if we have a real wedding."

"It won't be," Declan said.

She turned to look at him. "What do you mean?"

"Mom bought it," both women gaped at him. "What?"

"I was outside soaking up some sun when I heard her coming in. Followed her upstairs, where she was, not so quietly, trying to shove a garment bag in her closet. She said it was *the* dress. Willa glowed in it, and she needed to buy it."

Her heart started racing. She loved the dress and wanted it, but knowing Norah spent God knows how much money on it for the wedding that wasn't happening. She felt her heart sink at the thought of Norah wasting that money on something she wasn't sure she'd wear.

Declan brought his hand up to her shoulder and squeezed as she turned towards Talia. The guilt weighed heavily in her stomach.

"I knew Mom would do something like this," Talia said with a laugh. "She's been dying to help plan a wedding. And since she doesn't work, I think she's letting her excitement get the best of her. We'll figure this out, Willa."

Willa nodded but didn't say anything as Talia turned to leave the room, shutting the door behind her.

DECLAN PULLED WILLA into a hug as soon as the bedroom door shut.

She buried her face into his chest, letting out a shaky breath.

He pressed his lips to her hair. "I'm sorry. I should've known that something like this was going to happen. It's how mom operates." Declan ran his hand up and down her back, comforting her.

"It's—okay. I don't want your parents to feel obligated for something like this. Not when..." she trailed off.

"I know." He finished; his heart dropped. She nodded. He needed to work out whatever was stopping him from telling her how he felt. Maybe he needed a chat with Dempsey or Delaney when he was back in town. He knew Dempsey would give him shit for the situation, but he knew they'd be honest with him and help.

AFTER BEING REASSURED that Willa was okay helping Norah in the kitchen, Declan stepped outside where his dad stood, warming up the grill.

"Steaks as promised." He said, holding a plate of raw meat.

"Thanks, kid," Connor answered as he lifted the lid. As Connor tossed steaks on the grill, Declan shielded his eyes from the lowering sun, wishing he had brought his sunglasses out with him. Connor glanced at him and chuckled. "I forgot mine too."

Connor grabbed his beer and walked to the closest chair before sitting. Declan followed suit, placing the plate on the table in front of him.

"I'm thinking about building your mom a pergola for her birthday," Connor said, looking from the house to the sky above them.

"A pergola?" He asked, following his dad's gaze. He could see it—a dark-stained wood pergola, blocking most of the sun from view. "It would look really nice."

"Your mom's been hounding me for some shade out here for quite some time. I started it," he gestured to the posts in the ground. "But I've been pushing off finishing for no reason, but I think having you home this week would be a great time to knock it out. Dempsey said he doesn't have any classes on Wednesday and can swing by to help."

"What about Del?"

"He's going to try to make it back, but can't promise anything." *Right.* They were on the tail end of fire season on the West Coast, and Del was always the first on the plane to get there. How Connor and Norah made it through their day knowing what he and Del did for a living, he'd never know.

"I saw the Wyoming fire was ninety percent

contained. As long as there's no wind shift, I think he'll make it back no problem." He had to believe it.

"Always praying," Connor muttered. "Wednesday work for you though?"

"I've got no plans," Declan answered.

"Good. She's got a full day of appointments and errands, so she'll be out of the house." He took a drink of his beer. "Not sure about Willa, though."

"She'll be fine," he said. "We can put her to work if we need to."

"Put who to work?" Willa asked as she walked outside. "Norah sent me out for the plate. She saw the two of you lazing around. Her words, not mine."

"No, those words are too nice coming from you," Declan said, earning a glare from her and a shout of laughter from Connor.

"Oh, shut up." She smacked him as she sat down.

Connor lifted his beer to Willa in a salute. "Keep him in line. That second child, I'm tellin' ya. They're the worst."

"Excuse me," Declan feigned innocence. "I am an angel, okay."

"Right, and I'm a virgin." She rolled her eyes before she looked at Connor, changing the subject. "What are you guys doing Wednesday?"

"Going to finally finish this pergola for Norah. I started it a few years ago, but never got around to finishing it. Figured since her birthday is next week, it'll be a nice gift for her. Especially with the boys all being home." He smacked a hand on Declan's shoulder.

"Want to hang around and watch us get all hot and sweaty?" Declan asked, winking at her. He watched the blush creep across her face, as her eyes darkened ever so slightly at the idea. She might not love him in the way he loved her, but he knew her as well as he knew himself.

She bit her lip, confirming his thoughts.

"What's the matter? Cat got your tongue?" He quipped. His dad's laughter barely registered beside him.

Her green eyes locked on his. "Not around you, Dec. Your tongue isn't sharp enough to make a feline nervous." She retorted, a smug smile playing on her lips.

He leaned in and whispered in her ear so his dad didn't hear. "You sure about that? I remember the way you cried out for me that night. My tongue had to be sharp enough."

A quiet moan escaped her as he sat back, smirking. *Mission accomplished.*

"Si sa che un uomo bravo con la lingua è scarso a letto." A man who is good with his tongue is poor in bed, you know.

Declan ran his tongue along his teeth. Oh, she wanted to play dirty.

"Amore mio, non sapresti cosa ti ha colpito se ti portassi a letto." My love, you wouldn't know what hit you if I took you to bed. *"La tua dolce figa implorerà il mio cazzo."* Your sweet pussy will beg for my cock.

She squirmed, her face reddening as she glanced at Connor, who was busy on his phone.

When she locked eyes with him again, they were clear. Sharp. *"Come fa a sapere se sono un mendicante, Cazzo Piccolo?"* How would you know, small dick?

He huffed at her comment. He *tried* to know three years ago, before his life was turned upside down. He's had a handful of times since they arrived in Utah to find out.

"Lo saprò entro la fine del viaggio." He crossed his arms, mentally patting himself on the back for the Italian lessons. He *would* find out if she was a beggar before they were back in North Carolina.

Chapter Nineteen

"OF COURSE TODAY'S the hottest day of the week," Declan muttered as he walked towards the kitchen.

Willa sat at the island, deep in conversation with his parents. He leaned against the doorway, admiring the way she engaged with his parents. He couldn't get over how much she glowed as she talked to them. He loved how well she fit in with his family. It was as if she had known them her entire life, effortlessly fitting into their dynamic. Her passion for the subject at hand was contagious, and Declan found himself smiling as he watched her animated gestures and bright smile.

As he watched her, he couldn't shake the feeling of admiration and gratitude for having Willa in his life. She brought a sense of warmth and joy to every interaction, and seeing her conversing with his parents only solidified his feelings for her. She was beautiful, intelligent, and kind-hearted. He had always known he was lucky to have her in his life, even if he meddled his way in.

Right then, he decided that he was going to tell her. He wanted to take her out for a nice dinner, tell her how much he appreciated her, how much he truly loved her, how easily they could make this marriage work.

He pushed off the wall, and walked into the room, catching Willa's attention. She turned her attention to look at him, her smile widening. "Hey, you."

Declan cupped her cheeks and pressed his lips to hers. "Hey." He needed to kiss her more. She was intoxicating.

"Are you sure you don't want to come with me today?" Norah asked Willa. "I'm happy for some company."

Willa turned her attention back to Norah as Declan made his way around the island to grab a drink, pressing a kiss to his mom's cheek as he passed.

"I think a day to just relax is what I need," Willa said. "I've loved getting to see Bedpa, but I could definitely just use a day to do nothing. Maybe lie outside with my Kindle."

"Well, if you change your mind, you have my number." Norah looked at the clock on the stove. "I need to get going. I'll see you guys later."

Declan watched her kiss Connor before she turned towards him, pressing a kiss to his cheek. The gesture was used to embarrass him, but now he loved that she didn't care how old he was; he was going to get one regardless.

When the front door closed behind her, Connor clapped his hands together. "I have all the wood we need for the pergola in my truck at Pop's house. Dempsey is getting it now, bringing it over, and we'll get to work."

"Sounds good," Declan put his water on the counter before he left the kitchen to retrieve his shoes.

WILLA SAT ON the couch outside, kindle in hand. She was attempting to distract herself by reading the latest spicy Shain Rose novel, as the three men were engaged in a heated argument over the placement of a piece of wood.

She had watched as they affixed the pieces to the house, assembling the foundation of the pergola. Connor took charge, meticulously overseeing the process, while Dempsey and Declan firmly secured each piece, from opposite ends of the pergola.

The argument started when Connor misread his own handwriting, cutting a piece too short. She had learned that Declan was just like his father and older brother when it came to stubbornness. Add in the rising temperature, and the irritation was more prominent.

Declan was trying to diffuse the argument by changing the plans of the build to accommodate the piece, ensuring it wasn't going to go to waste.

She didn't know what it was about three grown men fighting, but she had to bury her face in a pillow on more than one occasion, so they wouldn't pick up on her fighting her laughter.

"I'm about to fucking go home," Dempsey grumbled as he pulled his Salt Lake Sirens baseball hat to pull off his sweat-soaked shirt, exposing more tattoos on his ribcage, his muscles rippling in the movement.

He tossed his shirt on the ground before running a hand through his damp hair.

The gesture had her shifting in her seat. Declan's gaze snapped from his brother to her as she did, heat flared in his eyes. *Oh shit.*

He shifted his body towards her, crossing his arms over his chest, cocking an eyebrow at her as he smirked. "What do you think we should do?"

Fuck.

"Oh yes, a woman's perspective is just what we need," Connor said, turning his attention to her.

She dropped her Kindle in her lap and slid her sunglasses off. *What was she going to say?* She looked at the pergola behind the men, feeling three sets of eyes on her. "Uhm—" *Fuck.* "Keep the original design, use the smaller pieces to make that side," she pointed to the far side of the pergola. "private. Your grandparents live there, right?" She gestured to the small blue house she could see from her spot on the couch.

"They do," Dempsey confirmed, before taking a big gulp of water.

"You're not shutting them out completely, but putting a privacy wall up right there gives you a little more of an intimate feeling. Perfect for a cool fall night."

Connor looked at the half-built pergola, then back to Willa. She bit her lip, nerves heavy in her stomach. He smiled at her. "That's a brilliant idea. Alright, let's get back to it." He said, grabbing the mis-cut wood from Declan.

Willa smiled at them, sliding her sunglasses back into place, happy to have this argument settled. Declan pulled his shirt over his head and tossed it on the ground before fixing his baseball hat. Seeing his toned muscles glistened with sweat. She sucked in a breath and knew he heard it when he smirked and winked at her.

"Does that really do it for you?" She jumped at the unexpected voice.

When she turned around, she found Delaney. His bright blue eyes sparkled in the golden afternoon sun as he gazed down at her.

When he sat, she wrapped her arms around him in a hug. "Back so soon?"

He shot her a grin. "What can I say, I'm just that good."

She rolled her eyes and sat back. "I'm glad you were safe."

"Always am, darlin'." He winked at her, which caused her to blush.

Why the fuck am I blushing? She only prayed that her face was flushed so he wouldn't notice. God only knows how much he'd hold *that* over her head.

"Get your own fiancée," Declan growled at his brother. "She's mine."

Mine. The word had her heart pumping harder.

Delaney arched an eyebrow. "We all know I'm the favorite."

"Like hell you are," Dempsey called out. "Just because you put out fires for a living doesn't make you the favorite."

"That's because I'm clearly the favorite," Declan commented.

Delaney opened his mouth to retort when Connor spoke up. "Will the three of you quit bickering. Del, get your ass over here and help like you said you would."

"See the shit I deal with?" Del stood, stretched. "Let's show these pussies how a real man works."

He pulled his shirt off and tossed it on the couch next to her, walking towards his father and oldest brother. She watched as he ignored the ladder and hauled himself to the top of the pergola.

"What a showoff," Declan muttered under his breath.

Willa laughed. "Why, Declan Matthew, are you *jealous*?"

He shot a look at her, one that could burn holes in a wall. "I do *not* get jealous. Especially at Del."

She shoved a finger in his side. "You're jealous."

He shifted and turned towards her, making her finger drag against his stomach. She didn't move her hand, completely in awe of his body—sweaty, toned. The way his muscles rippled beneath his skin, the sheen of sweat that glistened on his taut body. Her heart pounded in her chest; she felt breathless.

The heat of his skin felt scorching beneath her hand. She felt a rush of desire course through her veins. She wanted his hands on her, to feel the weight of his body pressed against hers.

He backed away from her suddenly.

He kept his sunglasses on, but she could feel his eyes on hers as he walked backward towards the pergola.

Willa chewed on her bottom lip before she broke, what she assumed was eye contact to focus on her Kindle and tried to read the words on her screen. Her mind drifted, thinking over their conversation from the other night. She wanted to know what he was like in bed. She had gotten a taste of it three years ago, and admittedly, she had that night on repeat whenever she had to take her release in her own hands. She knew that she'd beg for his cock if she ever got the chance.

She shifted in her seat, trying to ease the tension building in her core. She hadn't had sex since—God, she didn't even remember. She *needed* a release. *Fuck.* She couldn't sit here any longer. She thought about the toy Sofia slipped into her bag, hiding in its spot in the dresser.

No. Don't even go there.

But she didn't think her own hands could bring the release that she desperately needed, but the toy perhaps could. She needed Declan, needed his hands, needed the release that she knew he could give her as she screamed his name.

Fuck it. If she already had the damned thing, why not actually put it to use?

Willa closed her Kindle case slowly, trying to force her racing heart to slow down. She knew they couldn't hear the pounding, but she couldn't help but sneak a glance toward the men as she stood, slowly.

Once she was in the clear, she ran up the stairs, shutting the bedroom door behind her. She dropped her Kindle on the dresser before pulling open the middle drawer.

She grabbed the vibrator package and let out a sigh. "Are you really going to do this?" She muttered. "You're at his parents' house."

"Fucking do it already!" Declan's voice yelled through the open window across the hall.

Well, if that wasn't a sign, she didn't know what was.

Without thinking, she slid her shorts down her legs, kicking them off as she sat down on the bed, ripped open the box, and pulled the purple vibrator out. Her heart pounded as she lined the vibrator up to her entrance.

Do it. Do it. Do it.

Her mind was racing. She lay back as she pushed the purple toy in slowly, not missing how wet she already was from watching the guys work, how Declan growled *mine* at his brother. She was his, he just didn't know it.

She needed to come—deserved to come. She pictured Declan sliding his thick cock into her with ease, as she slid the vibrator into her for the first time.

She thought about his body, how tight and slick from sweat he was outside. Pressing the button and turning the vibrations on, she let out a gasp as it radiated throughout her body. The sensation was stronger than she expected, all of her senses heightening to a new level.

Thoughts of his hot lips on hers raced through her mind. She slid the vibrator in and out of her, increasing her speed as the vibrations began to increase in speed. Her skin tingled with anticipation, her muscles tensed with each wave of sensation, as if every inch of her was being awakened. She let out a moan as she felt the orgasm building, pushing her closer to the edge.

She bucked her hips as she rode the vibrator, imagined him between her legs again, remembering the feeling of his tongue and fingers as they explored her, igniting a fire within her. She thought about how he somehow knew exactly how to please her, how to make her body tremble with pleasure. His touch had been like a symphony, playing her body like a delicate instrument and coaxing the most exquisite sounds of ecstasy from her lips.

"Oh God," she moaned. She felt herself so close to that edge of release, where the tension was about to finally be relieved from her body.

Chapter Twenty

DECLAN NEEDED A break.

He didn't have an issue working outside, but he had worked up a big enough sweat that chugging water outside in the heat wasn't helping. What he needed was a minute in the cool air-conditioned house.

He also wanted to check on Willa. She had gotten up so awkwardly when she came in that he wanted to make sure she was doing okay. He called out for her a few times—when she didn't answer, he headed to the stairs, thinking she wanted to lie down. She tended to get tired when she got too hot. Walking up the stairs, he saw that his bedroom door was closed. *Odd*. He didn't think he shut it behind him earlier.

"Oh God."

The moan had him stopping at the top of the stairs.

"Please. Please. Please." Another moan. He stepped closer to the bedroom. "Dec. I need you so bad."

His grin was instant. Willa was clearly not *reading*, and he was definitely on her mind.

Declan grabbed the doorknob and took a breath before he pushed the door open.

The view that greeted him was something that was going to be forever burned into his brain—Willa, half-naked, one hand on a purple vibrator as she pleasured herself with it, and the other had such a tight grip on the bed sheets, her knuckles were white.

Her eyes were squeezed shut, lost in a fantasy. "Oh, Dec." She moaned again, as Declan watched Willa writhe on his bed as she moved the purple vibrator in and out. The way her spine arched as her tension built. He could feel himself go hard at the sight of her pleasure.

He could see the way her chest rose that she was close. But he wanted that orgasm. It was his. *Only* his.

He shut the door behind him, wanting to muffle any more sounds coming from his room.

"Why fantasize when you can have the real thing?" He asked, giving her the knowledge that he was there. What he *really* wanted to do was to go over to her and take care of her without a word, but knew he couldn't. Not this first time.

Willa's hand froze, and a moment later opened her eyes. He could barely make out the green of them; they were so dark, so full of need.

"Dec." She flushed and pressed the button to turn off the buzzing. "Oh God. I—"

"You what?" He leaned against the dresser, cocked an eyebrow. "I would *love* to hear you trying to talk yourself out of this one."

Willa's face turned red as she shifted in the bed. Oh, how he loved to watch her squirm. He knew she was partially embarrassed at being caught, but she had also caught right at the high before an orgasm. As he watched her hips rolling slightly, he knew she was trying to keep that high from leaving.

He pushed off the dresser and walked to the edge of the bed. She still had a knee up, her chest rising and falling heavily. The only sound in the room was her heavy breathing.

"Has it helped?" His voice came out huskier than he expected. *God, did he want her.* He wanted to lap her up and never stop. She shook her head. "Words, Willa."

"N—no." She stuttered out.

Declan climbed onto the bed and positioned himself at her knee. "Care for some help?"

He didn't wait for her answer this time. He reached for the purple toy that was still inserted inside her. He found the button, turned it on, and began to pump the vibrator in and out of her.

When his thumb found her clit, she let out a gasp as her back arched.

"Hmm, you like that." He said, more to himself than her. "All you had to do was ask."

He pulled the toy out and noticed the ridges on it, before he twisted it as he pushed it back into her, adding to the sensations, picking up the pace. He delighted in the way her hips kept rolling, trying to ride his every movement. Her moans became huskier, louder.

"Dec," she panted.

He reached a hand up and slid it up to her breast that threatened to come out of its place in her shirt. He needed his hands on her. Needed his mouth on her. He was desperate.

Without warning her, Declan pulled the toy out and tossed it on the bed beside them, as he affixed his mouth to her clit, sucking on it, plunging two fingers into her, feeling her slick walls as they squeezed around him.

He lapped at her, sucking, nipping, licking as her moans filled his senses. When she was close, he'd switch, never letting her quite reach that high. If this was his only chance to show her how they'd be together, then he'd make her go all night if he had to.

"Please." She begged.

"Implora per me, amore." He *craved* her pleas, her cries of pleasure.

He pulled away from her, both of them moaning in protest. Willa moved with him, leaned into him as he gripped the bottom of her tank top. "I need you, Willa."

"You—I—need—now," her words came out jumbled.

Declan ripped her top off, her breasts sat perked and ready to be devoured. "It's been three years too long," he said before he latched himself onto one, while he began twisting and pulling the other.

Willa's hand found his hardened cock through his shorts, rubbed along his entire length. He shifted and forced his way out of his clothing. He was wearing far too much; he felt like he was going to catch fire if it all didn't come off, now.

"Declan, please. I need you."

He slammed his lips against hers, eliciting a groan from her. He didn't care if he was being too rough, too needy. He *needed* her.

Willa leaned back as he pushed himself closer to her. His cock bumped against her entrance, the heat from it searing his blood.

"I'm not stopping this time." He said as he lined

himself up. He didn't ask about birth control; he knew she was on it, never missing a day to help with other issues.

"I'd kill you if you tried."

He wanted to press his lips to hers, to devour the gasp as she took all of him in, but he wasn't going to do that. He needed to hear her cry out for him. So instead, he buried his face in her neck and bit the sensitive skin as he slammed himself into her.

She cried out as he felt all the air in his lungs escape him.

He was so hard, so ready, he could come in three strokes. But he needed to make this last. He had waited too long for this moment; there was no way he was going to allow it to be over so soon.

"I can't believe I waited so long for this," she moaned.

Me too, love.

He began to move in long, deep thrusts. Groaning at the tightness, as he took them both to new levels of pleasure. Willa threw her head back as she arched into him. Declan latched his mouth onto her breast, flicking his tongue over her nipple.

"I'm close," she cried out.

Declan slowed down, his thrusts becoming painfully torturous. "Do you want to come or beg for more?"

Her green eyes opened and sucked him in. "Who says I can't do both?"

"What do you say, love?" he demanded, grazing his teeth along her collarbone, eliciting another moan out of her.

"Please. For the love of God." She pleaded.

"Your wish is my command," he growled as he thrust inside of her again. He wasn't going to be able to hold out much longer before he exploded. *"Mia moglie, amore mio."*

My wife, my love. Now. Always.

Once, twice, three more thrusts, and he exploded inside of her as she tightened around him, falling over the edge of ecstasy with him.

Declan dropped his body onto hers, their breaths coming out in ragged huffs.

"Holy shit." She said after some time.

He nodded but couldn't say the words. He was in heaven. He never wanted to move, never wanted to leave the comfort of her body.

He knew he would never be able to go another day without devouring her this way, again.

Willa rolled her hips underneath his, causing his cock to twitch inside her. "Round two already, love?"

WILLA FELT GOOD. As she lay in Declan's arms, she thought about how she hadn't been *this* satisfied after sex in a long time and had gone even longer without the mind-blowing sex she had just had—three times.

She sighed with contentment. Could her life really be so good?

Declan cleared his throat. "I uhm…"

She felt her heart tremble. This is when he told her it couldn't happen again. *Right*?

"You what?"

Worried, she shifted, sitting up to prop herself up on her elbow. She watched his expression go from lazy and content to panic.

"Oh, shit. No. I didn't—it's not. *Fuck.*" He dragged a hand through his hair. "It has nothing to do with what we just did. I *swear*."

"Okay," she said warily, unsure of what to expect.

"This is also completely the wrong time to do this, but I want to take you to meet someone tomorrow."

She arched an eyebrow. "This is the post-sex conversation you want to have?"

"Bad timing." He said sheepishly.

"You gotta work on that, Dec."

He leaned in to cup her cheek and kissed her. "I've been horrible about timing for seven years now." He pressed a kiss to her jawline. "Let me make it up to you."

Declan rotated them so he was on top of her, dragging his tongue and lips down her body, stopping only to swirl his tongue around her nipple.

"Declan, get your ass back downstairs," Dempsey shouted from downstairs.

She laughed and ran her fingers through his hair when he dropped his head on her stomach. "Why does everyone in this family like to cock block me?"

She pushed him off of her so they could both dress, stealing kisses as they went.

"They're all going to know what we just did." She stopped as they left the room, and a rush of embarrassment flooded her senses.

There was absolutely *no* way she could go back downstairs being flushed from sex.

Declan turned to her, "They know we've had sex before, Willa."

"Yeah, but like…that was *our* first time together." *Oh God, why was she like this?*

"Come on, love."

Chapter Twenty-One

THE NEXT MORNING, Willa woke up, satisfied from another night of lovemaking. She could really get used to the thoroughness that Declan possessed.

She rolled over to find the bed empty, but found a note from Declan in his place.

> Had to run out for a few things. Be ready for a day of play and an intimate evening.
>
> - Dec

How in the world was she supposed to dress for fun and—presumably—a nice dinner? Would she be allowed to change? Would they come back to the house to get ready? Why was he always so vague about his plans?

She rolled her eyes but felt a smile tugging at the corner of her lips. Grabbing her phone, she texted him.

WILLA

How the hell am I supposed to dress for today?

DEC

On a scale of 1-10, how annoyed are you?

WILLA

So you did this on purpose. I knew it.

I'm at 11. Dress code. Please.

DEC

Say the magic word

WILLA

I said please

DEC

… that's not it, love

Love. He had always called her that, but why did it make her stomach get all jittery?

WILLA

Declan.

DEC

Magic words

WILLA

If you don't tell me right now, I'm holding out.

She sent the text, pleased with herself. Despite being married and pretending to only be engaged, she loved the direction their relationship had taken. She only needed the guts to finally tell him how she was truly feeling.

When he didn't text back right away, she got a little worried and hoped she didn't overstep.

Putting her phone down, she got out of bed to head into the bathroom to shower. As soon as she turned the water on, she heard her phone ding.

She ran back into the bedroom, giddy as a teenager. *Lord, what was wrong with her?*

DEC

And how would you do that, Mia Moglie?

That nickname. She didn't know what it meant, and it was driving her fucking nuts. Whatever it was, it had her craving his touch.

WILLA

Well, you see, I have a dildo that could still keep me satisfied. What do you have?

She waited a few minutes for his response before she put her phone on the bathroom counter as she stripped naked. As she was stepping into the shower, she heard the familiar ding, checked it, and let out a laugh.

DEC

You're going to pay for that.

Willa's insides danced as she stepped into the shower.

DECLAN PULLED INTO the driveway of a charming two-story pale blue home. As Willa stepped out of the car, she took a moment to admire the neatly trimmed lawn and the vibrant flower garden that thrived in the crisp autumn air. When Declan offered his hand, she slipped her fingers into his, feeling a rush of warmth as they made their way up the steps to the porch.

Her palms began to sweat, and she heard Declan's faint chuckling. "I don't know why you're so nervous," he teased.

"I'm not," she protested weakly.

The porch was inviting, she thought, adorned with a white swing and two rustic wooden chairs. The front door, painted a bright red, stood out against the soft blue of the house. Willa's gaze lingered on a small chip in the paint—the smallest imperfection that seemed to signify the life within the home.

When Declan rang the doorbell, a chorus of shouting and barking erupted from inside, only to be silenced by the hurried footsteps approaching the door. Her heart raced in anticipation.

Who would answer? Who was significant enough to Declan—beyond his parents and siblings—to warrant this introduction?

When the door swung open, a stunning woman with dark, curly auburn hair answered the door. Her brown eyes lit up as she looked at Declan, and a smile spread across her face.

"Oh my goodness! You're back!" She dropped her hand from the door to wrap her arms around his shoulders. He let go of Willa's hand to return the hug. "I've missed you."

She felt a little out of place; she wasn't supposed to be here, right?

Stop that.

"I've missed you, too. How are you?" Declan asked when they broke the hug. He reached for Willa's hand again; her heart thumped in her chest.

"I'm okay. Good days and bad. I'm sure you know how that is." She turned her attention to Willa. "Hi. I'm Madeline, but you can call me Maddie."

"I—uhm…" *Get it together.* "I'm Willa."

Maddie beamed. "Declan has told me *so* much about you."

Willa smiled but didn't say anything. She couldn't remember a time he had ever mentioned someone named Maddie.

"Forgive me, please come in." Maddie stepped to the side. "I don't get many visitors these days, so my manners are not quite up to par."

Declan led the way in, pulling Willa in behind him.

The house smelled of lavender and lemon and felt as though Maddie had just finished cleaning.

Toys were scattered on the coffee table and hardwood floors.

"Where are the kids?" Declan asked as he pulled Willa to the blue sectional to sit.

"Millie is in the bathroom, and Porter went out back with the dog."

"Wait, Millie is potty trained already?"

Willa sat silently, clearly the outsider of the conversation.

"Hard to believe, right? She's my FOMO child. She hates being left out, but honestly, I'm not going to complain. I do not miss buying diapers, even if it means my baby is growing up."

Sadness flicked across her face, and Willa wondered if she wanted more kids but couldn't.

"Mama, I potty!" An angelic voice boomed into the living room, shortly before a toddler ran in, her brown curls bouncing. When she set her blue eyes on Declan, she stopped. "Dee!"

"Hey, baby girl!" Declan stood, picking up the girl to tickle her belly. Her laughter filled the room as she tried to stop him. "I have missed you."

"Yes, yes!" She shrieked in agreement.

"I have someone I want you to meet." He told her as he kissed her on the cheek. "This is Willa."

The laughter died from the girl's face as she locked eyes with Willa. "Hi there."

Willa felt *awkward*. She knew that this little girl was sizing her up. She clearly loved Declan, and Willa was stepping into her territory.

"Willa, this is Millie."

Millie. She wasn't why, sure, but the name suited her perfectly.

When Declan put Millie down, she walked over to her. Willa tensed, a little nervous.

"Hi!" Millie said after a moment, wrapping her arms around Willa's stomach.

Relief flooded her as she returned the hug.

"Mama, can I come back in?" A small voice shouted.

"Yes, honey. Uncle Declan is here." She called toward the back of the house.

"What?" Excitement flooded the voice as the door slammed shut. A brown-haired boy with the same piercing blue eyes entered the room as he ran straight for Declan.

Millie climbed into Willa's lap, clapping, as Declan lifted the boy upside down.

"Stop! Put me down!" the boy laughed, fighting to keep his shirt over his belly.

"When did you get so big, kid?" Declan asked, putting him safely back on his feet.

"I *am* almost five," he said, putting his hands on his hips, staring at Declan.

"You need to stop growing," Declan muttered. "I want you to meet my very special friend."

The boy turned his attention to her, giving her the same test that she was put under with Millie. Smiling, she said, "Hi. I'm Willa. What's your name?"

"Porter." His demeanor changed as he studied her. After a moment, he looked at his mom. "Can I go watch Toy Story?"

"Of course you can. Why don't you go get juice and some cheese sticks and take Millie with you?"

"Okay," he said, looking at Willa again before he turned to leave the room.

Something in her stomach told her he didn't like her, and for some strange reason, that hurt. She wanted him to like her, even if this was the only time she'd ever meet him.

Millie pressed a wet kiss to her cheek before she crawled off Willa's lap and hurried after Porter.

When they heard the refrigerator open, Maddie let out a breath. "Well, that was—"

"Very judgmental of the kid," Declan said with a laugh.

"I feel like I'm unwelcome here," Willa added with half a laugh.

"You're family, you're always welcome."

Family. Did she know? Willa turned her gaze to look at Declan, who answered the question with a shake of his head.

"So," Maddie continued. "I've learned from Delaney yesterday that you give Declan the rightful shit he deserves."

"The fuck?" Declan asked. "I do not deserve any shit."

Willa let out a laugh. This was her favorite kind of conversation.

"Excuse me? But yes, you do. How long have I known you?"

"A *very* long time."

Maddie shifted her attention to Willa now. "I'm a year younger than Parker and Declan, or the Linked Legends, as they liked to call themselves."

"It was cool."

"It was far from cool. No one had the heart to tell you otherwise."

"Whatever." He grumbled.

"Anyway, so I'm a year younger than them, and I could *not* for the life of me figure out who was who."

Confused, Willa asked, "What do you mean?"

"Has he never shown you a picture of them together?"

She shook her head. "I don't think so."

"Well, you'd know if he did. They were identical in every way possible."

"The only difference was our parents."

Maddie grabbed her phone off the coffee table, tapped, and scrolled until she found what she was looking for. She let out an *aha* when she found what she was looking for before she turned the phone sideways and handed it to Willa.

She didn't know what she expected, but what she looked at hadn't been it.

The photo was a slightly younger Declan with another man—who she assumed was Parker—each with their arm thrown around the other's shoulder. They looked like identical twins; she couldn't even tell which one was Declan. The same haircut, brown hair, and piercing blue eyes made them indistinguishable from one another. Even their facial structure was the same, from the gentle slope of their noses to the curve of their chins. Their eyes sparkled with mischief and humor.

"I can't even tell them apart." She muttered. The slightly taller one wore a grey T-shirt, while the other one wore a navy blue T-shirt, but even with these differences, she couldn't tell who was who.

"Parker is the one in the grey shirt," Maddie answered, giving her some insight into who she was looking at. She looked up at him. "It's eerie, isn't it?"

"Something like that."

"Parker and Declan were identical in every way, just short of having the same parents. Same birthday. Same year."

"Holy shit." She looked at the phone again, the

smiles on the screen mirrored the one she fell in love with. That much hadn't changed.

"Parker's mom, Connie, is Dad's little sister," Declan said. *Which explains why Parker has the Hawke features.* "They live in Maine. Moved there after Parker graduated high school."

"What happened to him?"

When neither said anything, she looked up from the phone. Maddie looked confused.

That's when it clicked.

Holy shit.

She looked at Declan. "I didn't know *that* Parker was your cousin!"

"I never told you?" Declan seemed as confused as Maddie.

"No! When we first met, you said that you joined the Air Force with your cousin, but never named him. Then when Parker—"

She trailed off, not wanting to say the words.

"It's okay," Maddie reassured her.

Willa nodded. "When the accident happened, you just kept saying Parker died, you needed to get home to help his family." She racked her memory and looked at Declan. "You mentioned Maddie and Porter. And a baby. I remember that. Oh God, I can't believe I never pieced it together. I feel so dumb now."

How could she never piece that together? She looked at Maddie. "I drove him to the airport after it happened. He just kept saying he needed to be home with his family. I assumed he was talking about Norah and Connor. Needing to be with them because he was struggling. I didn't assume—didn't think—that the family he was talking about was you."

She felt the shudder race through her. "I'm so sorry. I—"

Willa was so overwhelmed with emotion; she was on the verge of hyperventilating. Declan's arm wrapped around her as he pressed his lips to her head.

She wiped at a tear as it fell. "I'm sorry, it took me this long."

Maddie got up from her chair and sat next to Willa, pulling her in for a hug.

Why was she *comforting me?* Willa thought. She was the one who lost her husband. She was the one who had to raise two children alone. Willa pulled Maddie into her arms and held on tight. "I'm so sorry, Maddie."

She couldn't seem to say anything else.

Chapter Twenty-Two

THEY SPENT THE afternoon at Maddie's, getting to know her and the children better—Porter eventually warming up to Willa.

She learned about the shenanigans and schemes that Maddie witnessed as they grew up.

Maddie told her about how she always confused the two men, especially when they turned eleven, and decided to mess with everyone they knew and cut their hair in an identical style. The decision made them so completely identical that not even Norah or Connie could tell them who was who. Declan laughed and said that he spent three weeks living with his aunt and uncle until they decided to switch back, and none were the wiser.

Declan told her about when he decided he wanted to join the Air Force, how he was going to do it with Dempsey, but his brother decided to back out when he realized the military wasn't for him. When Parker got word of what Declan was doing, he jumped on board without a second thought.

She learned that Parker was the most selfless man Declan had ever met. He never wavered on his loyalty to his family—blood and made—his team, his country.

She couldn't help but shed a few tears as Declan told her about their time together.

Willa learned so much about Declan that she hadn't known, and she loved getting to know him through the eyes of someone like Maddie. Willa was dumbfounded that she had been able to keep herself together after losing her husband, especially while pregnant and already raising a kid. She was a remarkable woman, and Willa applauded her for everything.

Around four, they said their goodbyes, with promises to stop by again before they left town.

AN HOUR LATER, Declan parked the car once again in a small city called Claremore.

"What are we doing here?" She asked him.

"Well, the reservation for dinner isn't until six-thirty, so I figured we could walk around. Maybe do some shopping."

"Speaking my language," she joked as she nudged him.

"Come on," he said, grabbing her hand to link their fingers together.

She smiled at the gesture. He didn't *have* to, but it touched her that he was willing to walk around an unfamiliar city holding her hand like they were a real couple and not two friends who made a drunken decision.

She really needed to tell him how she felt. The

longer she went without doing so, the harder it felt to finally do it.

They came across a small boutique, full of bright colors and funky patterns. She ran her fingers over the fabrics, admiring the craftsmanship of the clothing. The shop owner had greeted them with a warm smile, pulling them into conversation on whether they were looking for anything in particular.

Willa found a few items she couldn't resist getting, with a few to take back to Sofia.

Checking out, Declan *insisted* on paying, and she argued that she could buy her own things. Eventually, they came to a compromise—he'd buy her clothes, and she'd buy the things for Sofia.

The next stop they entered was a small bookstore. Here, she knew, she'd get herself in trouble, silently thanking Declan for buying the clothes so she could spend that money on books. The smell of old books and the hushed quiet of the space enveloped her as she perused the shelves, running her fingers over the spines of novels and biographies. She came across The Divine Comedy, and a flash of Dempsey popped into her mind. She wanted to know what it was about this story that had captured his attention enough to tattoo it on his chest. Pulling it off the shelf, she cradled it in her arm, not missing Declan's eye roll, deciding she would dive into the world of Dante. She looked forward to the day she read it, so she could talk to Dempsey about it and her thoughts on the overall story.

They continued through the shop, pulling random books off the shelves, flipping through the pages, and reading bits of the stories. Some she put back, others she slipped into the basket she picked up to buy.

Declan snuck off to the restroom when she approached a woman sporting a python tattoo that wrapped around her right arm.

"I'm sorry, I'm not one to approach others, but I love that tattoo. It looked real."

The woman looked at her arm and then at Willa, her eyes so captivating that Willa felt envious.

"Thank you! I've had it for a few years now, and I'm absolutely obsessed. And between the two of us, my husband hates it, which makes me love it that much more." She let out a howl of laughter.

Willa's neck prickled, sensing Declan approaching.

The woman she was talking to shrieked with excitement. "Declan! It's so good to see you!"

He smiled and pulled her in for a quick hug. "I see you've met my fiancée." He put his arm around Willa.

Playing along.

"I'm Willa."

"It's nice to meet you, I'm Sienna." She looked at Declan. "How long are you in town?"

"Until Wednesday. I'm surprised Del didn't tell you." He looked at Willa. "Sienna and her husband, Austin, are Del's best friends."

"Well, Austin is. He's more of a pain in the ass for me." Sienna said, her tone joking, but her voice full of love.

She wondered if there was history or deeper feelings on Sienna's end. Her green eyes warmed as she commented on Delaney.

A laugh slipped out before she could stop it. "I can understand that one hundred percent."

"He told me the two of you got married last week. Was that true?"

Willa's eyes widened.

"That m—" Declan stopped himself. "*Please* tell me he didn't tell Austin."

"No. Del isn't that daft." She brushed at the tendril of black hair that hung in her face.

"Debatable." He muttered.

"Austin can't keep a secret to save his life," she told Willa. "But no. Del and I were texting when you were on your way back. He told me he convinced the two of you to elope."

"And that he did," Willa said.

"You weren't dating, right? Del said you're just friends."

What was she supposed to say to that?

"Not dating. But this married life isn't so bad, so we'll see what happens."

The words caught Willa off guard. Did he really feel that way, or was he just saying it?

The door to the bookstore opened, and Sienna looked past them to smile at the entering customer. "I need to get back to work. Are you ready to check out?"

"Yes, thank you."

As Sienna checked her out, she learned that she was the owner of the place.

They said their goodbyes and headed back to the car; they must've been in there longer than she thought. The sun had begun to set, and the streetlights flickered to life. "I never would have guessed she owned a bookstore."

Willa placed her bags in the trunk before Declan shut it, grabbing her hand. "She loves literature. She got really into reading freshman year because she had this massive crush on Dempsey."

She laughed as they began walking across the street. "You're kidding."

"Nope. If you asked her, she would tell you how she was madly in love with him and thought that the way to his heart was through books."

"I mean, she's not wrong, is she?"

Declan shot her a look. "No, I guess not. He wasn't into her. He was a senior at the time."

"Ahh, and seniors never looked twice at the underclassmen." She understood how that was, after how Sofia was in high school.

"Exactly. Then she met Delaney, who introduced her to Austin because he had a *very* jealous girlfriend at the time, and that was that."

They walked towards the bright lights of an Italian restaurant, Bella Luna. "Hungry?"

As if in response, her stomach grumbled. "Starved."

He laughed as he pulled the door open; the mouth-watering aroma of freshly baked bread, sizzling garlic, and olive oil welcomed them. The waiting area boasted a wall lined with carefully placed wine bottles, adding to the elegant ambiance.

She mentally patted herself on the back for opting to wear denim shorts and a loose-fit oversized t-shirt. She felt a little out of place with the way she was dressed now, but had she dressed in the t-shirt and athletic shorts she debated on, she would've been self-conscious here.

The door opened behind her, and she stepped slightly in front of Declan to let the new guests enter comfortably.

"Fancy meeting you here," came a male voice—he sounded so similar to Declan, but she knew exactly who it was.

Dempsey.

He wore an all-black ensemble. The sleeves of his dress shirt were rolled to his elbow, and one was casually thrown over the shoulders of a woman.

The woman was striking. She had gentle features—a small smile stretched across her full lips, and her hazel eyes bore a curious expression, silently questioning who Willa was and how she knew the man she was with. Her light brown hair cascaded down in loose waves, adding to her allure.

"Hey Dempsey," Willa said simultaneously with Declan. She looked at the woman, who seemed a little nervous.

"It's okay, il mio proibito," Dempsey said to her. *My forbidden.*

Why would he call her that? But something in her mind clicked.

She knew her eyes widened when Dempsey chuckled. He knew Italian, which only meant—

Oh. Oh, shit.

Humor filled his eyes. "I know all about you getting mom to call dad *small dick.*"

The woman threw her head back in laughter. "Oh

my God. Dempsey told me about that. I can't believe you guys are even okay with it."

"What they don't know, won't hurt them." He said. "This stays between us, okay? I know your secret; you know mine now."

Willa was confused, but he was right. Whatever it was, they could be considered even on secrets.

"This is Quinn, my girlfriend." She looked up at him, love filled her eyes. "This is my brother, Declan. And this is his wife, Willa."

"It's nice to meet you," Quinn said, smiling.

"Would you like to join us?" Declan asked.

Dempsey and Quinn exchanged a look before Dempsey said, "We'd love to."

THEY SETTLED INTO their meal comfortably, giving Quinn time to warm up to him and Willa.

He studied the couple across from him as he ate. They were comfortable together, while their eyes averted towards the room around them, as if they were in search of someone.

They learned that Quinn had a developmental psychology degree and that she was working towards her Master's, which is how she and Dempsey met.

Declan had a feeling that there was more to their meeting, but he didn't want to push.

Quinn opened up as she spoke about why she wanted to make a difference in the lives of children and their families. The passion and enthusiasm that radiated from her told him she was clearly in the right career.

Watching his brother and Quinn was eye-opening. After Dempsey's emotional dump the other day, he knew she was his person. He had always been more reserved and kept to himself, but around Quinn—he watched her with such intensity as if he needed to soak in every word she said. He knew that look had to have shown up on his own face when he got lost in Willa's words.

"Did you finally take her to meet Maddie today?" Dempsey asked him.

"I did."

"What he failed to tell me," Willa paused. "Well, what *I* failed to understand was that Parker was your cousin."

"You didn't tell her? What the hell is wrong with you?" Quinn smacked him on the arm. "What was that for?"

"I did tell her," Declan argued. "But I may have missed mentioning initially that my cousin I enlisted with was Parker, and after his death—"

He cleared his throat, feeling his inner demon stirring at the conversation.

"He mentioned the family, but I never pieced it together. Until today." Willa finished, understanding in her tone.

"This was your cousin who died on a deployment, right?" Quinn asked.

"It is," Dempsey answered. "I'll have to take you to meet her sometime."

Quinn's face lit up at the idea, telling Declan she was just as gone as his brother was.

Seeing them together, he wondered if Dempsey had told her how he felt yet, or if he had the same issue that Declan was having.

He glanced at Willa, who was finishing up her fettuccine alfredo. He needed to tell her everything.

Tonight was going to be that night.

THEY LEFT BELLA Luna, parting ways with Quinn and Dempsey, and started back towards the car.

They stood on the corner waiting for the traffic light to change so they could cross the street. The roads were busier now than they had been, as people made their way home from work or into town for a night out.

Declan took the opportunity to press his lips to the top of her head. She pulled back and looked him in the eye. He saw nothing but happiness and love in the deep green of her own.

Without a second thought, he leaned down, pressing his lips to hers, pouring everything into the kiss. She opened when he did, let him push his tongue into her mouth. She met him with equal emotion; all the unspoken words between them, the pent-up longing he felt, flooded through him.

He pulled back and cupped her face in his hands. He wanted to tell her he loved her, that he needed her to be with him, for real, to make this marriage work.

Grabbing her hand, he pulled her into the street to cross when they heard the screeching of tires as his world came crashing down.

Chapter Twenty-Three

THE JARRING SCREECH of tires sliced through the air, followed by the sickening thud that would etch itself into his memory forever. One moment, Willa was beside him, smiling, flushed, and holding his hand, and the next, she lay crumpled on the pavement, her body motionless, like a delicate porcelain doll discarded carelessly.

The sound of Willa's scream and his own echoed in the air, moments before the cacophony of sirens in the distance sounded, each note reverberating as an echo of lost moments he could never reclaim.

With every fiber of his being, he rushed to her side, his pulse pounding like a war drum in his ears. He knelt next to her, the world around him narrowing to the rhythm of her shallow breaths.

"Stay with me, Willa. Please," he pleaded, the imminent thought of losing her at the forefront of his mind.

His hands trembled as he desperately checked for a pulse, any flicker of hope. His mind wrestled with the tormenting memories of helplessness that crept closer like shadowy figures darting at the edges of his vision.

He hadn't known who made the call; his own panic had flooded his senses. It wasn't until he felt a hand on his shoulder, turning to find Dempsey and Quinn, that he realized they were probably responsible for getting medical attention.

Afraid to move her, he ran his hands over her head and her arms, needing the contact, willing her to be okay. He could hear the distant wail of sirens growing louder, inching closer as time felt like molasses.

Flashbacks of Parker lying lifelessly beside him, as blood trickled slowly out of his mouth and his ears. He could see Bennett lying on the sand in the same manner that Parker was—with Morris on his knees, his head dropped to Bennett's chest as he cried out.

The scent of hot metal, burning oil, of gunpowder mingled with the acrid residue of fear gripped his senses. His mind began to fracture, the boundaries between past and present blurring into an overwhelming haze of chaos. Each moment stretched into eternity as he wrestled with the ghosts of the past, their whispers urging him to surrender to despair.

"Breathe, Willa, just breathe," he urged, his voice cracking as he fought against the battle within him. The weight of his experiences threatened to drown him, but the most potent anchor was the bond he and Willa shared—an unwavering friendship that had bridged gaps, healed wounds, and now served as a thin lifeline pulling him back from the brink.

Dempsey pulled him back as the EMTs loaded Willa onto a gurney. He fought against his brother, unwilling to leave her.

"Family?" The large man asked.

"H-husband. I'm her husband." He said. "Please—"

The man nodded, allowing Declan to climb in. He grabbed her hand and refused to let go.

DECLAN FELT LOST.

If he closed his eyes, he swore he was transported back three years ago—could feel the sand under his hands, the hot desert sun beating down on his skin.

No matter what he did, he saw flashes of Willa turning into Parker, Parker into Bennett, and back to Willa. He could see the blood from each of them, unsure of who it belonged to.

He lost not one, but three of his own that day—Morris' mental and emotional state declined tremendously after that horrible day, ultimately giving in to the demons that hung over his head like a dark cloud. Declan held onto the pain and grief, the guilt that it was all his fault. He should've been paying attention; he should've *seen* the attack coming. He failed Parker and Bennett. He failed Morris.

And now, as he sat in the emergency room, he knew he had failed Willa.

Dempsey, Quinn, and Sienna sat with him in a waiting area, as Willa was wheeled away to receive whatever care she needed.

He didn't know how bad her injuries were, didn't know if she would come out alive.

He heard Willa's name being called and turned to see not only his parents and Delaney but Maddie too.

His family—by blood and choice—were all here.

He knew they would always show up, but something inside him snapped as Dempsey waved them over. The tears finally broke.

He didn't know how, but he was on his feet one moment and enveloped in his parents' embrace the next.

"Oh, Declan. We got here as soon as we could." Norah said, running her hand through his hair like she did when he was a child.

"Mom," his voice was so shaky.

He hadn't felt this way since Parker died, and in that time, it took him two months before he was even able to function properly.

If he lost Willa, he didn't know if he could recover.

He hadn't even told her he loved her. Hadn't told her he wanted to be with her. That he wanted to grow old with her.

And now he might not get the chance.

HE DIDN'T KNOW how much time had passed. He didn't ask, didn't want to know.

All he wanted was to know what was going on with Willa.

Every time a doctor or nurse opened the doors, he perked up, but they never stopped. Not for him.

He was so tired of the antiseptic scent that hung in the thick air, almost suffocating in its relentless sterility. His heart pounded like a drum in his chest, echoing the anxiety that gripped him.

He studied his hands as they trembled, while he fidgeted with the fabric of his shorts.

He studied his family individually.

His parents sat across from him—his mom rested

her head on her husband's shoulder as she read whatever romance novel she kept in her purse, while his dad scrolled on his phone.

Dempsey and Quinn sat next to him, whispering in hushed tones. He thought about how they must be feeling right now. He understood they wanted to keep their relationship a secret for whatever reasons they had, but here they were, waiting with him together. He knew that the family had questions, but no one dared ask them. Not when Willa's life was at stake.

Sienna and Del sat next to his parents, mirroring them. Sienna sat with her head on Del's shoulder, as they looked at his phone.

MINUTES HAD TURNED into what felt like eons, and just when he thought he might explode from the pressure of waiting, a doctor, clad in pale blue scrubs and an air of measured calm, entered the waiting area. Declan's heart raced, his throat tightening, once again, as he prepared himself. The doctor approached him, and for a moment, time stilled.

No words were spoken; it was the look on the doctor's face that would determine the shape of his world in that instant.

"Mister Hawke?" The doctor's voice was steady, with a touch of empathy, a knowing softness that made Declan's heart leap as he jumped out of his chair; his family, no doubt, followed suit.

Willa made it through surgery. The doctor articulated her condition, which felt clinical and distant. Declan understood she had some internal bleeding, a broken leg, a broken clavicle, and a mild concussion.

She needed time to heal, both physically and emotionally, but she was going to be fine.

A flood of emotion surged through him, releasing the tension that had coiled tightly in his chest. He could breathe again.

Willa was alive.

She was fine.

He lost track of how many times he imagined the worst, and now he felt the crushing weight of fear lift.

They were told to give them about thirty minutes before they could see her, and the doctor walked off to help the next family.

He felt his knees give out as the relief echoed deep in his soul. One of his brothers must have been standing beside him because he felt their arms wrap around him. He couldn't think past that she was okay.

His Willa.

Soon, he felt more arms and warmth, as his entire family wrapped around him in unison, and he couldn't think of anything else.

She was going to be fine.

Chapter Twenty-Four

WHEN WILLA OPENED her eyes, she had no idea where she was.

She took in the ceiling tiles, dimly lit up from a light behind her. She heard soft, rhythmic beeping to her left and turned her attention to the machines that showed oxygen levels, a heartbeat. She saw an IV bag hanging, watched it drip.

Was she in the hospital? What the hell?

She ran through the events of what had happened. She remembered dinner with Quinn and Dempsey. Saying goodbye to them after. The kiss.

Oh God, the kiss.

She remembered melting into him, feeling everything he poured into it for her, and what she gave him right back. *That* was a kiss between lovers, and it made her wonder if the shift she felt between them was real.

"You're awake," Declan's voice was hurried and raw, breaking her from her thoughts.

She turned her attention to him, smiling weakly. He stood next to her bed now. His usually lively blue eyes were dull and bloodshot. His gaze was a mixture of relief and anxiety. His hair was disheveled as if he had been running his hands through it for hours with worry —which he probably had.

"How are you feeling?" He asked before he scrunched up his face. She gave him a weak smile, understanding the question was absurd.

"Better than you," she joked, eliciting a smile from him. "You look rougher than I feel."

His eyes watered, filled with sadness. "I thought I was going to lose you."

"You can't get rid of me that easily." She said, smacking her lips a little. Her mouth felt like she had been sucking on cotton balls. "Can I get some water?"

"Shit, yeah." He grabbed a cup and held the straw to her mouth. She felt the icy cold water slide down her throat, sending a chill throughout her body.

When she was satisfied, she nodded. "Thank you," she paused. "The tires squealed. That's all I remember. What happened?"

His face became unreadable. "Ahh, well. One of the drivers had a heart attack while he was driving and swerved into oncoming traffic."

Willa gasped. "While driving?"

Declan nodded. "Unfortunately. The car that hit you reacted late and swerved towards us, hitting you."

"Oh," she chewed on her lip. "Are they okay?"

He gave her a quick smile that didn't quite reach his eyes. "Leave it to you. Yes, everyone is fine. The older gentleman who had the heart attack is still here. Not sure how severe his condition is since we're not family."

"And the other person?"

"I'm not sure. We haven't heard anything yet."

Willa nodded, unsure of what to say. "I hope they don't get into too much trouble."

"Willa, you were hit by a car."

"I know that, Dec. But the person who did it didn't do it maliciously. I don't want them getting into severe trouble for something out of their control."

Declan smiled then, a genuine smile that made her heart ache. "I love you; you know that? Here I am, worried sick about whether you were even going to make it out alive, and you're lying there thinking about the well-being of someone who put you here."

She stuck her tongue out at him, happy to see the humor on his face. "What happened to me?" She was too afraid to move, too afraid to see how bad the damage was.

"Broken fibula and clavicle. The doctor said you had some internal bleeding and a mild concussion."

She nodded, *not as bad as I thought.*

SHE DIDN'T REALIZE she had fallen asleep until Declan touched her arm, waking her up.

"Good morning, Miss Evans. I'm sorry to disturb you, but I just wanted to go over everything, instructions on proceeding, and get you out of here. Sound good?" The doctor said as he closed the door behind her.

"Sounds great. Thank you." She shifted in the bed, ready to hear whatever he had to say.

He walked her through everything—from the internal bleeding to post-operative care and recovery. It would take about ten to twelve weeks for her collarbone to heal, and since she didn't need surgery for her leg, he was recommending six weeks with no weight put on it. They wanted to monitor her for a few more hours and get her prescriptions in order before discharging her.

After the doctor left, Declan told her he had already reached out to her superior, informing her that Willa had been in an accident and would need to be put on convalescent leave, and that they would work out the details once they got back to North Carolina. He also told her he called her dad and left a voicemail letting him know what had happened.

Declan's phone had to be silenced at one point, once he informed his family that she was awake and doing well. He told her that Norah was already making preparations to make her as comfortable as possible once she returned to the house.

The fact that his family was willing to help make sure she was comfortable. She wasn't used to that, didn't know how to react to it.

Dempsey and Quinn stopped by, dropping off the rental car, just minutes before a nurse came into her room to get her discharged.

Declan helped her into the car and drove cautiously —the most cautious she had ever known him to drive— and got them back to his parents' home.

Norah fussed over her—something else Willa wasn't used to—meticulously checking on her pillows, bringing snacks and drinks, ensuring that Willa had everything she needed.

Declan refused to leave her side, his presence a steady anchor amid the whirlwind of emotions that surrounded her. He sat on the bed couch with her, holding her hand, while whispering reassurances in her ear.

She noticed he was on the verge of tears the entire day, and had no doubt that thoughts about Parker, the demons that came with his PTSD, played a role.

Connor returned home with white calla lilies and a gallon of cookie dough ice cream after Declan had told him it was Willa's favorite flavor.

Maddie brought the kids over, both kids carrying daisies, with Sienna following closely after, holding her own bouquet of tiger lilies and pink tulips. The last had been a surprising visit, and Willa had decided she wanted to get to know the bookstore owner a little more later on.

Norah invited both to stay for dinner, stating that the situation called for all of their loved ones to be close. Life was too short.

Eventually, Dempsey walked in carrying five pizza boxes, with Quinn carrying bouquets of sunflowers and yellow roses. Dempsey told Willa that an impromptu gathering was enough to keep Norah busy and maybe have her fussing over Willa less. Especially with Porter and Millie in the house.

She felt overwhelmed with love and gratitude from Declan's family, truly feeling like one of them as they doted on her. From her seat on the couch, she watched the conversation between Quinn and Norah, how comfortable they both seemed, and wondered if they had talked while she was in the hospital.

The front door opened again, announcing Delaney's arrival.

"Have no fear, the fun is here!"

The house filled with a mixture of laughter and groans. He walked through the house, beaming like he was king of the world.

He too brought flowers, a bouquet of colorful tulips, sitting them on the island next to the other flowers. Willa couldn't help but smile at how full and bright the kitchen looked with all the flowers.

Delaney made his way around the kitchen, kissing all the women on the cheek as he went, before he plopped himself on the couch beside Willa.

He slung an arm over her and pressed a kiss to her cheek. "You know, if you had married me, like you *should* have, this," Delaney gestured to her leg. "Wouldn't have happened."

Declan muttered something under his breath, which had Willa reaching over to grab his hand again.

"Seriously, though, we can get you a quick annulment and run off together."

Willa couldn't hold off her laughter. "Sounds good to me, handsome."

Declan groaned. "She's *mine.* Back the fuck off, Delaney."

Del tsked. "My, my. Someone is touchy. You're a little too territorial over someone who's just a friend."

Willa looked at Declan as he shot Delaney a glare. She didn't know what was going on between them, but a piece of her felt a little smug that they were fighting over her.

"She's *my wife.*"

Shivers tore through her body at the words. Where *was* this territorial side coming from?

Del simply smirked at his brother, like he had won a bet she was unaware of.

"Then prove it," was all he said.

THEY DIDN'T SPEAK much as Willa got ready for bed, not that he knew what to say anyway.

She was tired. A combination of what had happened yesterday, all the visitors today, and the medications she was sent home with just wiped her out.

While she showered, he set up her side of the bed, giving her a few extra pillows for elevation, and putting ice water on the table alongside her pain medication.

Between the flashbacks with Parker, Willa's accident, and all the panic and worry he felt over the last twenty-four hours, he was amazed that he was still fighting his inner demons. A part of him wanted to cave, let it pull him under, even temporarily, knowing that he was the reason for the deaths, for allowing Willa to get hurt the way she did.

But the other part—the stronger part—knew that he needed to be strong. Not just for himself, but for Willa.

She was the love of his life, and he was not going to let his demons take him from her.

Once she was settled in bed, he cupped her chin,

dropped his mouth to hers. He kept it simple and sweet, despite the need to pour everything into the kiss.

"Text me if you need anything."

She smiled softly as she settled into the bed, her eyes heavy with sleep already. "I will, but I will be fine. You've taken good care of me today, Dec. Go spend time with your family."

He hesitated but nodded. "I love you, *Mia Moglie*."

She was asleep before she could answer.

AS DECLAN WALKED downstairs, he found Maddie at the front door, holding it open for Del to carry a sleeping Millie to their vehicle.

"Heading out?" He asked.

"Yeah. We stayed later than I intended. Dempsey is getting Porter. He passed out in the backyard."

Declan chuckled. "Sounds like him." He waited a beat, watched as Dempsey carried Porter through the house. "Need any help?"

Maddie smiled at him. She looked good, despite everything that happened. Declan knew she was fighting her own internal battles, but she was resilient, and she would always come out on top.

"Del and Dempsey got me covered, but thanks."

He didn't know why, but something in him needed to know. "You're doing okay, right?"

"I'm still here, aren't I? Look, I know it hasn't been easy. Not for me, the kids. I know it hasn't been easy on you. Don't let those demons win, okay? You have such an amazing support system here with your family. With

Willa. Don't lose that." She reached for his hand and squeezed. "Whatever is going on between you and her —tell her. She deserves to know. You never know when something is going to drastically change that. You deserve to be happy."

"I am happy," he argued.

"Sure, you're happy, but your happiness is not what it used to be. I know you still hold Parker's death over your head like a cloud. It wasn't your fault. No one blames you for his death. I certainly never have. The kids will never do that, because there's some comfort in knowing their favorite uncle was with their daddy. I know you well enough to say that I *know* you haven't told her how you really feel because something inside of you says you don't deserve it."

"That's—" *true*. He could admit to himself day in and day out that he was in love with Willa and needed to tell her, but something stopped him. Something *always* stopped him.

Maddie cocked an eyebrow at him. "See, that right there tells me I'm right." She pulled him in for a hug. "Be happy, Declan. It's what Parker would've wanted. You deserve that kind of love and happiness."

With that, she turned and headed for the car where her sleeping children waited. He watched her hug Dempsey, then Del, before she slid into the driver's seat and headed home.

She was right.

The only thing that held him back from telling Willa how he felt was himself. Maybe he hadn't come to terms with that reason being the guilt he felt over Parker, Bennett, and Morris. How, out of the four of them, was he the only one who still walked this earth? He was happy, sure, but he got in the way of his own happiness. That, he knew, was letting the demons win.

And he couldn't let that happen anymore.

His brothers approached the house, stopping just inside the door where he stood.

"Problem?" Dempsey asked.

"No," he said. "No problem. But I think I'm going to need both of your help tomorrow. If you can spare me some time in the morning?"

"I'm free. Quinn and I have plans, but if it's early enough, I can probably make it work."

Del shrugged. "I got nothing but time. What do you have in mind?"

Chapter Twenty-Five

DECLAN TOOK ONE last look around the backyard and decided it was as perfect as it was going to get.

Thanks to Del, of all people, he had connections to a local florist and sweet-talked the owner into opening hours early just for them, so they could get this done.

Declan and his brothers carefully arranged roses and lilies—both in shades of red and white—the image of Willa's reaction was the driving force behind the decision. He knew in his heart this was the perfect setup for this. Her favorite flower combination, in his favorite place.

"Everything is squared away," Del said, coming to stand next to Declan, clapping a hand on his shoulder in reassurance. "Looks good, brother."

"Think she's going to like it? Or feel the same way?" He knew there was something different in their relationship, but he just didn't know to what extent. *What if this wasn't enough? What if she didn't feel the same way?*

"Stop worrying," Dempsey said. "If she didn't feel the same way as you did, she wouldn't have gone with that idiot's plan."

"You mean genius," Del commented.

"Whatever." Dempsey turned his attention to

Declan, crossing his arms. "She wouldn't have done it. You said that you sobered up pretty quickly after the decision was made, right?"

"I did," he said, and he had. He remembered their wedding as well as he remembered his birthday.

"What makes you think she didn't do the same?"

Declan opened his mouth but shut it. Maybe his brother was right. *Could* she have faked it, just like he did?

"She's going to love it. I'm just glad it took *my* idea for you to fucking do something about it."

"I was getting there; you just pushed the idea along sooner," Declan grumbled.

"I'm good like that. Aren't I, Dempsey?" Del asked, fixing the lapels of a jacket he wasn't wearing.

Dempsey was quiet for a while, long enough for Declan to glance his way. His brother looked a little annoyed, but eventually dropped his arms. "Unfortunately. If only you weren't blind to your own feelings." He patted Declan's shoulder. "I gotta get out of here. Let me know how it goes."

"I will, thanks." He said.

After the door shut, Del looked at Declan. "What did he mean by that?"

"By what?" Declan asked as he fidgeted with the flowers again.

"If only you weren't blind to your own feelings."

Declan looked at his little brother, the confusion evident on his face. "Do you ever question yourself on why you hang around with Austin and Sienna so much?"

"No? Why would I?"

"Try sitting down and figuring it out sometime. The answer is right there in your face."

"You and Dempsey have lost your fucking minds. I'm going to head out. Got plans today." He could see it, though in his brother's eyes, the soft realization that he wasn't fully ready to admit. *One day, he'll see it for real.*

Declan nodded. "Thank you for helping, too. Could not have done this without you."

"I know," was all Del said before he strolled out.

When he was alone, Declan smiled. The Hawke brothers were in big fucking trouble.

DECLAN FELT TOO impatient waiting for Willa to wake, so he decided on a shower. He needed to shake the nervousness, or he was going to fumble the entire thing.

After he had dried off and changed into a pair of khaki shorts and a nicer shirt he found in his closet, he went into the bedroom to check on Willa, only to find the bed empty.

His heart stammered in his chest. "Shit." He ran out of the room, scraping his shoulder against the door frame. "Fuck."

He stopped halfway down the stairs to rub at his shoulder when he caught sight of a crutch at the back door. He wanted to take her out there himself, to be able to watch her face when she took everything in.

But, if being in the military had taught him anything, it was how to handle when the plan changed. He could still make this perfect. For her, for *them*.

Heart pounding with urgency, Declan ran down the last of the stairs, through the kitchen, and came to an abrupt stop as he stepped outside. He swore in that moment that his heart stopped. Willa stood amidst the vibrant sea of red and white flowers, their delicate petals glowing in the soft golden light of the setting sun. The sky above was painted in hues of orange and purple, casting a warm, romantic glow.

Even in her matching pajamas and casted leg, she looked radiant. She always did.

He loved this woman so fucking much, and it was time she knew it.

He closed the distance between, slowly, taking the time to absorb the scene before him, burning it to memory. No matter the outcome, he'd never forget how she looked at this moment.

"Hi." He said, coming up behind her.

"What is all of this?" she asked, her voice soft and full of emotion.

He smiled, the scents of the flowers mixing with the faint scent of her peach soap had his eyes wanting to roll back in his head. He wished he could bottle the smell and preserve it forever.

"Well, I *was* going to do this big romantic gesture where I carried you outside. You know, broken leg and all."

"Ever the romantic," she joked. "Sorry, I ruined that for you. Want me to go back inside so we can try again?"

"See. That's one of the things I love about you. You get injured and can take a joke. You don't pity yourself. You just roll with it."

"If you can't laugh at yourself," she started. "So, are you going to tell me what this is about?"

His heart pounded in his chest. "I cannot believe I get to do this while you're in your pajamas. But I wouldn't have it any other way."

"What are you talking about?"

"Do you need to sit?" He asked.

"No, thank you."

"Good," he grabbed her left hand, and ran his thumb over the sapphire ring on her finger. "I love you."

"I love you too, Dec. But—"

"No, hold on. I don't just love you, Willa. I'm *in* love with you." He felt the smug smile slide across his face at her sharp intake of breath. "You are the first thought on my mind when I wake up and the last before I fall asleep. My heart races at the mere sight of you, and your smile lights up my darkest days. When I'm with you, I find a sense of peace and happiness I have never known before. Your kindness, your laughter, and the way you view the world have captivated me in ways I cannot fully explain. Every moment with you feels like a dream I never want to end."

He heard his voice shake, but kept going. He needed the words out there. He gripped her hands tighter and looked her in the eye. Made sure she knew he was being serious. "I love the way you make me laugh, the way you listen, and the way you care for those you're around. I love that you've pulled yourself from the trenches more than once, and I have loved the courage and strength you have to do that. From the moment we met, something inside me changed, and I am more thankful for that and you, every time my eyes open to a new day. I have been in love with you from the very beginning. Whether you take me as a friend or lover, I'm just happy to know you the way I do."

"Dec," Willa's face was streaked with tears. "I'm in love with you, too. Truly, madly."

He couldn't believe what he was hearing. The woman he had been in love with all these years loved him back. He felt a rush of emotions—joy, disbelief, and a deep sense of relief that she felt the same way. "You mean that?"

Tears marked her cheeks as she smiled at him. "If I weren't in love with you, I don't think I would've gotten married to you."

Dempsey's earlier comment popped into his head. "How drunk were you when we got married?"

"I sobered up the minute Del mentioned it."

"Son of a bitch," he muttered. "Will you do this with me? I know that would mean we skip over dating, over an actual engagement, but—"

"Declan. I don't care about all of that. You've been mine for a long time. I want that, permanently."

"You'll always have me," he said.

"No," she shook her head. "I need you in my life. I need you in my bed. I need to know that every morning I wake up, you're beside me."

"Are you sure because—"

"Will you just shut up and kiss me already?"

Without a moment's hesitation, he leaned in and pressed his lips to hers, sealing the deal.

Epilogue

One Year Later

FOUR HEADS TURNED when the doors to the bridal suite burst open.

Willa let out a breath when she found her sister-in-law, Taelyn, running into the room, arms full of bags, her brown hair still slightly damp and tousled from a recent shower. She was wearing the black silk pajamas and fuzzy slippers Willa had gifted the bridesmaids.

"I am *so* sorry. I lost track of time, and then I ran into Lu Me Suli downstairs, and now I'm just flustered." She dropped the bags and let out a breath.

Willa had no idea what *lu me suli* stood for; since her vocabulary only expanded to some Italian.

"Who is that?" Willa asked. She had spent the last year getting to know all of Declan's family better, but Taelyn was the one sibling who rarely came home.

"An ex," Taelyn said as Talia pulled her into a chair and began to pull her hair back into a Dutch braid.

"Oh," Willa nodded, sliding a glance at Sofia and Quinn. "Can we get a little insight on who this is?" Aside from Declan's siblings, Sofia's family, and her dad, she didn't really know anyone else—the main reason she wanted to keep the wedding small.

"Atlas Pavlina," Talia said, loosening up the braid strands on Taelyn's hair.

"Dempsey's best friend?" Willa needed to get her dress on, but she was so engrossed in learning about Taelyn and Atlas, she needed to know more. She *loved* the drama.

"Oh, I smell drama," Sofia chimed in. Willa glared at her best friend. "What? We all know dating your brother's best friend is a recipe for drama. How long were you two together?"

"We started dating my second year of college. He was in his first year of grad school." Taelyn looked at Quinn through the mirror. "Perks of going to a college away from home is being able to have relationships without family finding out."

"How did Dempsey take it?" Quinn asked.

Taelyn was silent for a moment. "He didn't know; no one in the family knew."

"I only found out because when they broke up, I happened to go to Tae's apartment to surprise her for a sister's weekend and she was..." She trailed off.

Understanding and sympathy filled the room. "I'm sorry," Taelyn said, shifting in her seat. Talia pulled the last of her hair back into a bun at the base of her neck. "Happy day. No more conversations about an ex."

Something in Taelyn's eyes told Willa there was more to the story, but she'd drop it. For now.

"All done, sis," Talia said, squeezing Taelyn's shoulders. "Remember, there's an open bar. Get drunk, then go fuck him," she said with a wink before she shook her hips.

"Alright, we need to get moving," Sofia said. "You have a man to marry—again."

DRESSED, WILLA PACED in the room. She was nervous and excited—the anticipation that had built had her on edge. She watched Quinn double-check the dusty blue dresses, ensuring that everything was in its place.

She didn't know why she was so nervous. Today was their first anniversary—not that anyone outside of Declan's siblings and a select few others knew that.

"How much longer?" Talia asked, standing in front of the full-length mirror. Willa mentally patted herself on the back for the dusty blue dresses. The color brought out the warmth of Talia's eyes and complemented her sun-kissed skin. The fabric hugged her curves, the gentle flow of the skirt, and the delicate lace details that adorned the bodice.

"Henry should be here any minute," Sofia confirmed, checking her phone. "We're on schedule."

When the knock came at the door, Willa practically pounced, but was stopped by Quinn. "I got it."

She opened the door. "Hey, Henry. Looking good."

Willa watched as her dad stepped in, hand on his stomach, wearing a tailored black suit. "You look nice as well, Quinn."

"Thank you. I'm going to step out for a minute. Be back," she said as she slipped out of the room. Willa knew she was off to find her own fiancée and didn't blame her one bit. She wished she could sneak off by herself and find Declan, but he had remained firm in not seeing her until she walked down the aisle. He wanted to do something traditional when it came to their relationship.

Henry turned his attention to Willa, his deep brown eyes reflecting love and pride. Even a year later, she was still a little shocked when she could read emotion on her father's face.

After she healed from the accident, she and Declan visited her dad to tell him they were getting married. When they arrived at his house, Willa was taken aback to find that he not only had a serious girlfriend of his own but that she was getting him to branch out and not be the stiff person he was raised to be. Willa didn't know Eva very well, but she was grateful for the woman who changed her father.

Henry's face brightened as he smiled, the first real smile she had ever seen from him. "You look…" he trailed off, clearing his throat. "Absolutely beautiful."

She smiled as she crossed the room, wrapping her arms around him. "Thank you. That means the world to me."

"Are you ready?" He asked as she pulled away from him.

"Beyond. It's been a long time coming."

"I'm proud of you. I know I don't tell you that as often as I should, but I am." Willa's eyes filled with tears. She blinked them back and prayed they wouldn't fall.

A knock came at the door, immediately followed by Quinn's popping through the door when she opened it. "It's time to go."

Willa nodded, taking a shaky breath. She had been dreaming of the big, white wedding since she was a little girl, but it was finally being here, knowing Declan was at the end of that aisle waiting—even being with him for a year still had her nerves on edge. But she was ready. "Let's do this."

DECLAN WAS SO nervous to see Willa that he couldn't stop his hands from sweating. The decision to *get married* on their anniversary was a fun inside decision, but the wait was agonizing. He had been so worked up, feeling like this day was never going to come, and now that it had, he needed it to be done, so he could be with his wife, his Willa.

Wiley Terrell, an old friend of his dad's who offered to officiate the wedding, stood next to him as they waited for the wedding party to start their march down the aisle. This was it, the moment he had been waiting for; he didn't want to be away from her any longer than necessary.

Soft instrumental music began to play, signaling the bridal party. Declan stood with bated breath as he watched Max, Parker's younger brother, making his way down the aisle in a grey suit. After living abroad for the last five years, Max returned to support Maddie and her children. Coping differently after Parker's death, Max eventually reached out to Declan to learn the full story. Their bond grew stronger after Declan flew to London to meet with him. On his arm was Quinn, in a timeless and graceful silhouette. Her figure was complemented by the sweetheart neckline and cinched waistline of her dress, flowing gracefully around her ankles as she walked. She held a delicate bouquet of white lilies and roses, a reminder of how far he had come with Willa. Anticipation coiled tight in his chest as he watched them, excitement rising with every heartbeat.

One down.

Cruz and Taelyn followed. Taelyn's dusty blue dress resembled Quinn's, but hers was adorned with tiny sequins that shimmered in the sunlight, twinkling like stars in the night sky. Declan noticed her gaze shift towards the right side of the guests as she walked, straightening with every step. He mentally noted to ask her about that later.

Talia and Delaney followed, Talia in the same dress as Quinn. As she separated from Del, she deviated from her path, playfully approached Declan, and pulled him into a quick hug. "Love you, Dec."

He kissed her cheek as she pulled away. "Love you too, Clingerella." She rolled her eyes at the nickname she had been dubbed for twenty-three years now.

Dempsey and Sofia began their walk down the aisle, where Sofia's gleaming dress caught the sunlight just like Taelyn's did. Giving him a wink as she separated from Dempsey, who leaned into Dec's ear as he stood in his place, "Ready?"

"More than you could understand." He muttered.

"Understatement of the year," Dempsey said. Declan didn't need to look at his brother to know that his gaze slid down the line of bridesmaids to his fiancée.

The music shifted, and the guest rose to watch as Henry and Willa walked towards the aisle. Declan's heart began pounding in his chest.

Henry came into view and then—*Willa*.

Declan swore his heart stopped the moment he caught sight of Willa. The A-line dress his mom had purchased last year was simply stunning, and on her, it was—breathtaking. The dress hugged her figure in all the right places, accentuating her curves and making her look radiant. The off-the-shoulder design drew attention to her delicate collarbones and graceful neck—both of which he couldn't wait to get his mouth on.

As she walked towards him, her eyes shining with happiness and excitement, he couldn't help but marvel at how perfect the dress suited her. The perfect blend of classic and modern, just like Willa herself. The wait to get her in his arms again felt like an eternity.

When she reached the end of the aisle, he felt a surge of emotion. Seeing her standing there, in all her glory, was a moment he would remember for the rest of his life. When she turned to Henry, Declan noticed the slit in her dress and swore he was going to give Vivi the biggest kiss he'd ever given someone for blessing that dress with that slit.

Declan reached for Willa's hand when she offered it, allowing Henry to step back towards his seat next to

Eva. "You look beautiful." They stood in position and allowed Wiley to begin.

He had no idea what Wiley said. Declan waited to say his vows, lost in the whirlwind of emotions and thoughts. He felt his heart beating rapidly, his palms clammy as they held Willa's, and a lump formed in his throat. He watched Willa, refusing to take his eyes off her.

"Declan, your vows," Wiley said, breaking him from his thoughts.

"Right," he cleared his throat and prayed he wouldn't forget what he wanted to say. "Willa—from the moment our paths crossed, I knew my life would never be the same. Your love has been a beacon of light, guiding me through the darkest times and illuminating the brightest moments. Being with you feels like coming home, a place where I can be my true self." He took a breath, steadying his voice. "You have a way of making everything around you beautiful, and your kindness and warmth inspire me to be a better person. I cherish every moment we spend together, and the thought of you alone brings joy to my heart like nothing else."

He squeezed her hands when he saw a tear spill over. "I vow to cherish and respect you, to care for and protect you, to comfort and encourage you, and to stand by your side no matter what challenges we face. I promise to be patient, kind, and understanding. To listen with an open heart and mind, and to always speak the truth with love. Together, we will build a life filled with laughter, adventure, and unwavering support. I will celebrate your triumphs and comfort you in your sorrows." He paused. "Willa, you are my best friend, my confidant, and my one true love. I choose you today and every day, forever and always. With all my heart, I give you my love, now and for all the days of our lives."

She reached up and wiped the tears that fell.

"Willa?" Wiley asked with a quiet voice.

She nodded and let out a breath before looking into his eyes. "I don't know how I'm going to follow that." She muttered, getting a small chuckle from the guests. "Declan—I struggle to find the words to describe what you mean to me. From the moment I met you, I knew that you were the one for me. You have shown me what true love is, and I am grateful for every moment we have shared. You've shown me a love that is profound, unwavering, and full of joy. I vow to stand by your side through all of life's challenges and triumphs, pulling you from the trenches when you need me to. I promise to support you, encourage you, and be there whenever you need me. I will always be your partner, your confidant, and your best friend. I promise to love you unconditionally, to be faithful and true. I will be your rock, your safe haven. With all that I am and all that I have, I give you my heart, my soul, and my love."

Tears fell from Declan's eyes as her words sank in. Her words touched him in a way he hadn't expected. As he looked into her eyes, he saw a depth of emotion and vulnerability that he had never seen before.

He longed for their future with her, longed for the life they started together, filled with love and companionship.

They exchanged rings—hers a simple diamond

band, keeping the sapphire of her engagement ring the focal point, while his was a simple black stone band. He was going to miss the simple silver band they exchanged last year, but Willa insisted on him getting something better, something that fit him better.

Wiley pronounced them as husband and wife. Declan wasted no time pulling Willa into his arms, pressing his lips to hers, and the world around them faded away.

All that mattered was the love they shared and the promise they made together. When they separated, he kissed her again, whispering, "My love. *Mia Moglie.*"

Bonus Epilogue

Two Years Later

"WHEN WILL MADDIE be here?" Willa asked when Declan walked into the room, her eyes not budging from the front door. After knowing her for over ten years, he knew that she was worrying herself over this.

He glanced at the clock on the living room wall. "She should be here in about five minutes."

Willa nodded, biting her lip nervously. He hated that she was nervous. Since they moved to Utah last year, she had become close to Maddie and knew Willa considered her one of her closest friends.

She needed that, though. Sofia and Cruz still lived in North Carolina, and they talked regularly, but the two-hour time zone difference and individual families really messed with their communication.

Declan walked to his wife, brushing a thumb over her bottom lip, releasing it from her teeth. "You'll be fine."

"What if she's not happy with our decision?"

"Why wouldn't she be?"

"We're honoring Parker. Besides," he sat down on the couch beside her, their newborn daughter snuggled in his arms. "Our Parker is a girl."

Willa's face lit up as she scooted closer to him. He

pressed his lips to her forehead before he looked down at their baby.

Declan couldn't believe that he finally got the life he dreamed of. He was married to his best friend, had the house of his dreams, was serving his twenty in the military, and now had the perfect little family.

He really couldn't ask for more.

When Willa opened her mouth to talk, the doorbell rang. Declan stood up, handing Parker over before he pressed his lips to Willa's. "I love you. I love Parker. Maddie is going to be thrilled, so there's nothing to worry about, okay?"

"Okay," Willa whispered before she dropped her eyes to look at their daughter.

Declan pulled his phone out and snapped a quick photo so he could send it to Willa later. He was determined to have as many pictures of her with their daughter as she was bound to have of him with her.

He pulled open the front door and smiled. "Hey, Mads!"

Maddie's face lit up. "Hey, Dad. How are you?"

Dad. He felt surreal hearing that.

"Tired, but fantastic. I didn't know that this is what life could feel like." He pulled Maddie in for a quick hug.

"It only gets more tiring, but so much better," she said, walking into the house.

"Where's Porter and Millie?"

"Porter is at baseball practice, and Millie is in gymnastics. Del said he's picking them up to bring them over. He wants to see the baby, too."

Declan snorted a laugh. "As if he hasn't been here

every day for the last week, harassing Willa and the baby."

"Well, let's hope he finally grows a pair and makes his situation with Sienna permanent soon. He needs a baby of his own to leave the rest of the Hawkes alone."

Declan laughed. Delaney and Talia were the only ones who didn't have any children, although he was sure that Talia and Benedict would be having a kid within the year now that they were married.

"I think we both know Sienna is going to have to be the one to make that first move."

Maddie laughed in agreement. "Now, where's this baby?" Declan motioned for her to follow.

He made his way into the living room to his wife and daughter, his heart swelling in his chest.

Declan walked behind the couch to stand at Willa's back, as Maddie walked in front, tears forming in her brown eyes.

"Oh my goodness!" She leaned down to give Willa a one-armed hug. "How are you doing, momma?"

"On cloud nine," Willa answered, as Maddie sat on the couch next to her. "Come meet the newest Parker."

Maddie's eyes widened. "What?"

Declan smiled when his cousin's eyes met his. "Her name is Parker Grace."

"Oh my," She wiped at a tear before she took the baby from Willa. "Look how precious you are, Parker Grace. Absolutely perfect."

"KNOCK, KNOCK," DELANEY called out as he opened the side door.

"Hey," Declan said from the kitchen.

Willa heard the brothers talking, assumingly to Porter and Millie, speaking in hushed voices. She turned back to Maddie, who was holding a sleeping Parker.

"I hope you're okay with—"

Maddie held up a hand. "I swear, Willa Hawke, if you don't finish that sentence with 'cuddling one of the most perfect babies', I *will* smack you."

Willa let out a huff of air. She knew she was going to be called out, but she wanted to make sure that Maddie was okay with them using Parker's name.

"Look, I understand why you're nervous. I wish you had met Parks. He was amazing in every sense of the word. Just because he died doesn't mean we can't let his legacy live on."

"You're sure, though?" She asked before biting her lip nervously.

Maddie laughed, patting Willa's knee. "I love it, honestly. She has a beautiful family, and she'll make her own destiny with that name. As for my Parker—I can promise you if anything, that man probably has a God complex because there's a baby in the family named after him."

Willa nodded. She hated that she was so nervous—so unsure—on how Declan's family would react to her. Sure, in the last three years, she's felt more at home than she ever had, but she was always afraid that one wrong thing she said or did would have her booted from the family.

Declan came into the room, guiding the six-year-old Porter into the room by his shoulders, with Delaney behind them, holding hands with five-year-old Millie.

"Is that the baby?" Millie whisper-yelled.

"It is. You need to be super gentle with her, okay?" Declan said.

Both kids nodded before they walked to their mom.

"Meet your new cousin, Parker." She said, shifting her body so her children could look at the baby.

"Parker…like Daddy?" Porter asked, his voice shaky.

Willa's heart ached at the emotion she heard in Porter's voice. She couldn't imagine what was going through his head right now. She only hoped he was just as okay with it as Maddie and the rest of the family had been.

"Can—can I hold her?"

Before Maddie could respond, Declan squatted next to him. "You have to sit down and be very careful with her, okay?"

Porter nodded before he climbed onto the couch between Willa and his mom. Declan positioned his arms before he nodded, giving Porter and Maddie the go-ahead to hand the baby over.

When Parker was settled into his arms, she opened her eyes briefly, the bright Hawke blue stared back at Porter before she closed them again, smacking her lips as she fell back to sleep.

Porter surprised Willa by leaning in, pressing his lips gently to her forehead before he said, "I'll protect you like my daddy would've protected me, Parker. You can count on it."

Maddie sniffled, trying to contain her emotions, while Willa wiped at a tear. Needing a second, she got up off the couch, with help from Declan, before she walked towards the bathroom for some cold water to splash on her face.

WHEN SHE WALKED out of the bathroom, she found Del poking his head in her refrigerator.

"What are you doing?" She asked, causing him to jump.

Del turned, his mouth full of an apple, while he held two more in his hands. He gestured to the island. Willa rolled her eyes as she opened up the cabinet that held her cutting boards before she placed one on the white marble countertop.

Del saluted her with an apple before he placed it on the cutting board. Willa grabbed two plastic bowls she kept on hand whenever kids came to visit and placed them on the counter beside the apples.

They were silent as Del chewed on his apple while he cut the apples up for the kids.

"I'm proud of you, Wills."

"Aww. Look who's getting soft on me," she joked.

"I am not," he said, lifting his black t-shirt to show off his abs. "The only person going soft around here is Declan. He's gotta get that dadbod going."

"You wish. The military specifically won't let that happen."

Del huffed. "But seriously. That baby is probably the cutest one I've seen."

"You said the same thing after Amara *and* Theo were born." She countered, bringing up Taelyn's daughter and Dempsey's son.

"Yeah, but I'm telling the truth this time."

"Oh, shut up. You'll be saying the same thing in a year or two when Talia has a baby, and then you'll never say it again once you finally get your head out of your ass and start making babies with Sienna."

His eyes glazed over. "We're not even dating."

"That's right. You're *just* roommates." Willa said with an eye roll. How the man still hadn't admitted his feelings to the woman and did something about it was beyond her. Sure, that might make her a hypocrite, but at least she and Declan didn't live together, complicating the relationship.

"Will all of you stop harping on me about Sienna so much? She's not interested in me in that way. She never has been and never will. She has Nyla to focus on. So leave it alone. I think I'm just destined to be alone forever, and I'm okay with that."

She hurt for him, for the words he spoke. In no way did she believe that Sienna wasn't interested in Delaney in that manner, but the situation—the divorce and friendship Del had with Austin at one point—fucked that up for both of them. She just hoped that one of them would get the courage to do what everyone knew was the right thing for both of them.

"I'm sorry, Del. We just want you happy."

Del's shoulders sagged before he dragged a hand through his hair. "Don't apologize. I've just…" he paused, clearly trying to find the right words. "I just have a lot on my mind lately. But I'm not here about my love life or lack thereof. I'm here for you, Declan, and my newest niece."

Del pulled her in for a hug, one he clearly needed. They held each other, listening to Maddie and Declan talk to the kids in the living room.

"Do you need anything?" He asked when they pulled apart.

"No, I think we're good," she said, and meant it.

Del nodded before he kissed her cheek, then grabbed both bowls of apples and walked into the living room.

Willa sighed as she grabbed the cutting board and knife, placing them into the sink. She grabbed a bottle of water from the refrigerator and headed toward her family.

When she entered the room, she stopped, grabbing her phone from her pocket to snap a photo, to remember this moment.

If it wasn't for Sofia dragging her sorry ass to Club Thirst, she never would've met Declan. If she hadn't met Declan, she wouldn't have gotten married while she was half drunk, and her life wouldn't be what it is today.

She couldn't believe that this was her life now. She went from a lonely life as an only child to marrying into one of the best families she had ever met. She had everything she had ever wanted, and that was something to be thankful for.

Acknowledgments

I jumped into *Camouflage Hearts* so fast after finishing *Of Wind and Shadows* that I had absolutely no direction for this story. What started as a dream, turned into this book and I'll forever be thankful for that.

To my husband, Ed, for supporting me in my life-long dream of writing, and walking me through scenarios I needed for this book. I love you, always. <3

To my friend and alpha, Jade, for sticking with me throughout the writing of this story, anxiously waiting for the next chapter, and for yelling at me during certain points of this book because I was breaking your heart as I do.

To my Beta readers who gave me the feedback I needed, you helped me make this book what it is today.

A special shoutout to Klara-Mei and Jules for being not only my Betas, but buddy reading *Camouflage Hearts* together, compiling their list, and giving me some of the best feedback I was given—and an even more special shoutout to Jules herself, for convincing me to add in the car accident.

About the *Author*

Devon Cook was born and raised in Northeast Indiana and currently resides in Chesapeake, Virginia with her husband and four children. She is a stay-at-home mom who helps families book their dream vacations. In her spare time, you can find her with a book in hand or laptop open as she loses herself in another world.